Join up [illegible] dn't Timmy think of that before? At last [illegible] n have a rest from all those amorous exploits. And what an opportunity to get away from scheming Sid and the rest of the Lea family.

But not a chance! There are lots of excitable ladies at The Royal Loamshire Regiment, including the physical W.R.A.C.s who prey upon impressionable soldier boys. And if that is not enough, Sidney arrives to entertain the troops. It is all very distressing . . .

. . . And very funny too. Timothy Lea's latest adventures match up to his previous unputdownable sexploits.

Also by Timothy Lea and available from Sphere Books

CONFESSIONS OF A WINDOW CLEANER
CONFESSIONS OF A DRIVING INSTRUCTOR
CONFESSIONS FROM A HOLIDAY CAMP
CONFESSIONS FROM A HOTEL
CONFESSIONS OF A TRAVELLING SALESMAN
CONFESSIONS OF A FILM EXTRA
CONFESSIONS FROM THE CLINK

Confessions of a Private Soldier

TIMOTHY LEA

SPHERE BOOKS LIMITED
30/32 Gray's Inn Road, London WC1X 8JL

First published in Great Britain by Sphere Books Ltd 1974

TRADE
MARK

Set in Times Roman

Printed in Great Britain by
Hazell Watson & Viney Ltd
Aylesbury, Bucks

ISBN 0 7221 9328 9

CONTENTS

CHAPTER ONE

I'll never know how I managed to end up in the army. I mean, of all the professions I never thought of going into, the army was the one I never thought of going into most.

I never even reckoned it on the telly. All those adverts showing blokes leaping in and out of jeeps and on the point of having it away with W.R.A.C.s who looked like Raquel Welch. They never convinced me. What about all the geezers who can't be there because they've snuffed it? That's what I used to ask myself. I bet all these other countries have got commercials showing the bright side: you know, killing people. Somebody has got to come out second best. There has got to be a moment when chatting up birds over the white-hot top of your steaming sub-machine gun has got to stop. And then it's, pouf, you're dead. And not only the poufs either. Blokes like you and me. And with my luck, especially me.

Of course, I suppose, coming out of the nick had a lot to do with it. Even in these emancipated, 'anything goes' days there is still a faint stigma attached to being chucked into the chokey. Especially if it is for flashing your full frontals in a filthy film. The fact that I lost my remission for taking part in an orgy before the assembled inmates of Penhurst Prison did not help very much either. I could say a lot in my own defence but I find the subject too painful to dwell upon and can only commend interested readers to consult *Confessions from the Clink* for the full and sordid details.

Anyway, I was at a very low ebb when I eventually staggered away from Penhurst, not least because of the physical deprivations I had been forced to endure. Putting it another way: I had not had my end away for three months. The early days when Penhurst had been a haven for do-gooders and good doers were long past and successive governors seemed to be vying with each other to bring new stringency to the penal system. As for me I was very worried about my own penal system, if you know what I mean. Three months is a long time to a healthy lad who likes throwing it about, and I was not at all certain that the four-fingered widow was an adequate substitute for what I had been missing.

When it was time to go the Governor said a few words about keeping my nose clean – I don't think he was really referring to my nose – and I was pushed out with my train fare home. At least it would have been my train fare home two weeks before when they put the fares up. In the end I have to hitch-hike home and I am not in a particularly sparkling frame of mind when I eventually bang on the front door of 17, Scraggs Lane, ancestral home of the Leas. The minute I have done this I turn sideways and wait for Mum to pull back the curtains of the bay window. Mum knows that there are a lot of funny people about – after all, she married one of them – and she does not believe in taking chances. This suits Dad who has no wish to communicate with the outside world, most of which he owes money to.

Two minutes later Mum's mug peers suspiciously through the lace curtains and settles into a resigned smile of welcome. I am disturbed to find that she blushes when she sees me and it occurs to me that my performance on the stage in Penhurst Prison still lingers strongly in her mind. How anybody could have mistaken cannabis for spinach I – and, no doubt, the two ladies I was appearing with – will never know.

'Hello, dear,' she says, opening the door and looking nervously up and down the street. 'You're looking very thin. Are you all right?'

'Fine, Mum,' I said, stepping uninvited into the house. 'The old pile hasn't changed much.'

'Well they don't. Not unless you have the operation and I don't fancy it at my age.'

'I didn't mean that,' I said hurriedly. Blimey, I love my

old Mum but she is as thick as a set of cork table mats. If you don't spell everything out in words of one syllable she will always get you wrong. 'I was talking about the house. It's just the same.' This is not strictly true because the heap of junk that Dad has nicked from the lost property office is even larger than usual and swollen by an imposing selection of gas masks, some of them as recent as World War II. Should the Chinese decide to attack with gas, 17, Scraggs Lane should be one of the last dwellings to succumb to the Yellow Peril.

'I don't know how people go on having this stuff to lose,' I say. Mum nods her head in agreement.

'Your father hates to see anything going to waste, that's the trouble. Every time they have a sort out down at the office he brings it all back here.' Mum's use of the word office is significant. She reckons it sounds posher to refer to her old man as working at 'the office' rather than 'the lost property office'. Mum is a bit of a social climber on the side and for that reason, if no other, my latest lapse must have been a very choking experience for her.

'How's Dad taken it?' I ask.

Unfortunately I am staring at the harpoon gun when I speak and Mum is swift to take the opportunity to misunderstand me.

'The usual way. Slipped it under his mac. Didn't you read about it in the papers?'

'What happened, Ma?'

'It went off in the tube and pinned him to the ceiling.'

'Ooh! Ma! Was he all right?'

'He didn't suffer any physical injury. Some ruffians took advantage of his situation to steal his wallet and undo his braces.'

'That's not nice, Mum.'

'It was terrible. He thought they were trying to release him and then they suddenly got out at Clapham North and left him with his trousers round his ankles. He couldn't move 'til the train got to Morden.'

'Didn't anyone else try and help him?'

'No. He said they all took one look at him and went in the next compartment.'

Diabolical, isn't it? Still, I suppose, when you think about it, it's not every day you see a bloke pinned to the roof of a tube train by a steel bolt with his trousers round his ankles. It could give you a bit of a turn, couldn't it? Not the kind of thing to send you home whistling if you were escorting your best bird back from the Granada, Tooting.

'How is Sidney?' I ask, eager to switch the conversation from my mother's unfashionable ailment and father's misfortunes.

For the uninitiated I had better explain that Sidney Noggett is my poxy brother-in-law and a frequent contributor to most of the misfortunes that befall me. He has an unpleasant habit of coming out of every situation smelling of violets whilst the odour that surrounds me is of a rather more earthy nature.

'You should see him soon,' says Mum. 'He said he'd pop in before dinner.'

'What's he doing now? Still in clubs, is he?'

'I don't know, dear. You'd better ask him. It seems to change so often I can't keep up.'

That does not surprise me. Sidney's business ventures are seldom of the long-term variety. Either bankruptcy or the police – or sometimes both in a muck sweat, dead heat – always seem to catch up with him.

'And Rosie and the kids?'

'They're very well. Rosie is going to dancing classes.'

'She's left it a bit late, hasn't she?'

'Not ordinary kind of dancing. This is all about finding the Zen or something.'

'What was that, Mum?'

'It's no good talking to me. You'll have to ask her. She should be here later.'

Sister Rosie has been becoming more and more of a handful since she started reading the colour supplements and watching BBC 2 and I am not surprised to hear that she is into some new kind of self-exploration kick.

'Every Thursday, down at the British Legion Hall. They get a very nice class of person there. They've all got little French cars.'

I can imagine. It is always the ones who should know better who get tired of pottery classes first. Before you know where you are they are doing 'O' level French and knitting red, white and blue mittens for the laundry man. After that it's anything goes and the privet eaten down to navel level by the milkman's horse.

Rosie was always a bit of a raver but in the old days she had the decency to feel guilty about the way she was carrying on. Now she reckons that she has the same right to get her end away as a bloke. Disgusting, isn't it? I feel a lot of sympathy for Sidney. In fact I think it is one of the things that keeps us together. I mean, if us blokes don't stand shoulder to shoulder and stick up for our rights we could find ourselves in the same situation as the Yanks: millions of bigmouthed women trampling all over us.

'Where are they living, now?' I ask.

'Vauxhall. Rosie wanted to be near the West End. They bought an old house and gutted it. Must have cost them a fortune.'

I feel like pointing out that it cost Sidney a fortune but I do not pursue the matter. Deep down, where no one in his right mind would dream of looking, I know that Mum is a woman, and they are basically all the same.

'I told them they were fools,' says Mum. 'Do you remember when they had that lovely place at Streatham? I never knew why they gave that up.'

'Because Sidney was skint at the time. He goes up and

down like a blooming yo-yo. You don't want to worry about Vauxhall, Mum, it's very fashionable at the moment. It's going up.'

'Most of what I've seen is coming down,' sniffs Mum. Poor old thing. She doesn't understand that all the nobs are fighting to live in places that the people who live there are fighting to get out of. She would reckon she had moved into Westminster Abbey if you offered her a flat in Wimbledon. She does not realise that people want to be near the art galleries and theatres and all the other places they never go to because there is something on the telly.

'The kids all right, are they?'

Mum's face assumes the expression of doting joy that is always reserved for her disgusting grandchildren.

'Jason is doing ballet now.'

'Blimey. Is Rosie trying to turn him into a poufdah? They haven't given up hopes of having a girl have they?'

'He's got a natural bent, that child,' says Mum, reproachfully.

'That's what's worrying me. I haven't forgotten him on that diabolical telly programme.'

'I don't want to hear a word against little Jason,' Mum gives a tell-tale sniff. 'At least he hasn't broken his mother's heart yet.'

'Yes, yes,' I say hurriedly. 'And talking of heartbreak, how's Dad? Hard at it as usual, I suppose?'

'No need to be sarcastical,' chides Mum. 'Your father hasn't been very well lately. One of his old war wounds has been playing up.'

Quite what my father did in the war has always been something of a mystery to me. Fire watching has been mentioned but I think it was mainly the one burning in the grate of 17, Scraggs Lane. Certainly I don't think he ever traded bullets with the enemy. Cigarette cards, maybe, but not bullets.

'What injury, Mum? Writer's cramp from trying to get his post war credits?'

'Don't mock,' says Mum, coldly. 'You're in no position to point the finger. You haven't exactly brought lustre to the family name.'

'Lustre' is a most unusual word for my mother to use and I can only assume that she lifted it from a furniture polish advert on the box. I got my education that way.

'I know, Mum,' I say, humbly. 'I'm going to try and make amends.'

I mean it too. I know I have been a disappointment to my parents since I first got done for nicking lead, diabolical decision though it was. I saw three fellows loading lead on to a lorry and they asked me if I would give them a hand. Said they were collecting for the church roof. Trouble was that they were stripping the lead off the church hall. Not knowing the religious landscape of the parish – and being a bit of a twit into the bargain – I was the mug who landed up in the South Western Magistrates' Court.

I am about to enquire after Dad's whereabouts when the man himself appears as Mum makes a discreet exit. He emerges from the kitchen clutching the carved up copies of the TV Times which serve as bog paper in the Lea mansion. I think it advisable to point out that Dad has been doing his stuff in the outside throne room beyond the kitchen and not – no, you could never have thought that, could you? Still, I suppose if you knew Dad as well as – no, it doesn't matter. Anyway, there he is: five foot ten and a half inches of temporarily relieved depression centred over South West London. He looks down at my legs as if he expects to find a ball and chain around one of them and tosses his head contemptuously. I wonder if he is going to make his joke about 'the return of the prod-it-all son' but he restrains himself.

'So you're back, are you?' Is this all he can manage?

'I think you said that last time, Dad.'

'What do you expect? The bleeding poet lariat reading an address of welcome?' Dad shakes his head bitterly. 'I suppose you've come back to bring more shame about our heads.'

'I don't know about "our heads", Dad,' I hear myself saying. 'It's certainly a shame about your head. The rest of you isn't so good either.' The minute I close my mouth I know that I have spoken foolishly but, somehow, with Dad, I don't seem to be able to restrain myself. He really does know how to get up my bracket to beyond the hair line.

'You cheeky little basket!' he snarls. 'No sooner inside the door than you're at it. I don't know how you have the gall to come back here. This isn't the Prisoners' Aid Society.'

'I'm sorry, Dad,' I say, controlling myself with difficulty. 'I don't know what came over me. I didn't mean to be rude. The words just jumped into my mouth.'

'Well, next time, swallow them before they jump out again. If you're going to stay around here you'd better learn a bit of respect.'

'Yes, Dad.'

'You nearly broke your old mother's heart, you know.'

'Yes, Dad. She was hinting at it.'

'She was a blooming sight more than hinting at it to me, I can tell you. I had to put up with her day and night. It nearly drove me round the bend.'

'Yes, Dad.'

'Talk about paying a debt to society. I reckon I footed your bill while you were in there. My taxes subsidised you. All that and your mother going on the whole time.'

'Yes, Dad.' He does make a meal of it, doesn't he? It must be like a holiday down at the Lost Property Office when he doesn't show up. I don't know how Mum puts up with it.

'I hear you've been having a bit of your old trouble,' I say, deciding the time has come to change the subject and demonstrate a bit of concern for the miserable old git.

Dad looks at the bog paper. 'I think it was the sausages

we had last night. I don't know what they put in them these days.'

'I didn't mean that, Dad,' I say, patiently. 'Mum was saying your wound had been playing up.'

'I've had a few twinges,' says Dad, putting on his 'I fought through Hell and lived' face.

'You want to take it easy, Dad.'

Nature's greatest argument for compulsory patricide looks up sharply.

'Are you trying to take the mickey?'

'No, Dad. I—'

'I do my bit. I always have done. Not like some people. Some people don't know what I've been through. The doctor said he'd never seen anything like it. He didn't know how I kept it up. "You're a walking miracle" that's what he said to me. He'd never met anyone with my willpower, you see. I don't talk about it much but me and pain are not strangers. Oh, dear me, no. I don't let on much but—'

'Yes, Dad,' I say, trying to halt the flow before he really gets going. 'You don't have to tell me.' Not again, I must have heard it a hundred times.

Luckily Mum announces that tea is up and I am spared any more details of how Dad is going to romp away with the Martyr Of The Year Award. Not that the alternative is all that great. Mum's Rosie Lee certainly brings out the gypsy in me and what can you say for a woman who cannot even make a decent cup of tea? I can remember when she used to open the tea bags and pour them into the pot. What with one thing and another it does not take me long to get the feeling that 17, Scraggs Lane has not got a lot to recommend it over the nick.

'Have you got a job lined up?' asks Dad.

'Give us a chance, I only got – I only came home this morning. I didn't call in at the Labour on the way.'

'You don't even know where it is,' says Dad scornfully. 'I think I'll buy you a street map so you don't get lost.'

'Perhaps Sidney can find something for him,' says Mum.

I am swift to shake my head. 'No. I'm going to stand on my own two legs. Nothing Sidney has lined up for me has ever worked out. Not in the long term, anyway.'

'That's not all Sidney's fault,' says Mum, wagging a finger at me. 'I have to speak as I find even if blood is thicker than water.'

'I don't care if it's thicker than melted nougat,' I say. 'I don't reckon that it's an accident that Wonder Sid has cleaned up the ackers while I've been cleaning out the "D" Block khasi.'

It is at this propitious moment that there is a quick 'We are the champions' on the door bell and I prepare to greet my poxy brother-in-law as Mum goes off to do a recce through the lace curtains.

'Hello, Timmo!' says Sid a few moments later. 'I didn't know you were coming out today.'

'Didn't you get a telegram from Buckingham Palace?'

'I didn't bother to read it. I thought it must be another bleeding garden party.'

'Sidney!' says Mum, shocked. As far as she is concerned there is nothing to choose between God and the Duke of Edinburgh. Probably not a lot to choose as far as the Duke of Edinburgh is concerned. I am not really taking a lot of notice because I am drinking in Sid's clobber. He is wearing a black serge safari jacket and matching trousers with a raised seam. It is all very trendy and makes him look a bit of a poufdah. Not at all the Sid I remember back in his faded denim days.

'He's not looking too bad, is he, Mum?' says Sid. 'He needs a bit of your home cooking to fatten him up.' Sid winks at me and I give him my 'do us a favour' look. Mum cooks like she has a pathological hatred of food and is trying to pay it back for some injury it has done her in the past.

'I've got a nice bread pudding planned for this evening,'

she says, proudly, as I wince. I make a better bread pudding when I'm mixing paste to go fishing.

'How's the family?' I ask.

'Smashing. Rosie should be over with the kids in a few minutes. Tell you what. Why don't you and I slip out for a couple of jars and then we can look in later. There's not room for us all in here. You fancy a beer, do you?'

'Great idea, Sid. Let's go up The Highwayman.'

'Don't go drinking too much,' warns Mum.

'There's no danger of that. Not with those two buying!' says Dad who is about as tight as a gnome's foreskin when it comes to lashing out for a round of drinks.

When we get to The Highwayman I hardly recognise the place. There is piped muzak, a snack bar and everything tarted up with the most diabolical wall paper. It quite puts you off your ale. Not that this commodity is very easy to come by anyway, and when I ask for a packet of crisps the geezer behind the bar looks at me as if I have been trying to force my hampton through the slit in the Doctor Barnado box.

'We don't do crisps,' he says witheringly. 'You can have a toasted sandwich.' He indicates a fish tank bearing the word 'Toastimat', inside which are littered a few melting blobs which remind me of the scene three feet below a vulture's perch. The sight is not calculated to have me diving into my pocket for 30p.

'Let's go in the garden,' I say.

'Kiddies only,' says the barman sharply.

'But there aren't any kids here.'

'That's the rule. If you don't like it—' He keeps looking me up and down as if he is trying to tell me something.

'The place has changed a bit, hasn't it?' I say to Sid. 'I don't recognise any of the old faces.' It is a fact that all the birds look as if they have just had their hair done and the blokes are wearing ties. One or two of them even have suits on.

'There's a lot of middle class people around here, now, Timmo,' says Sid. 'You get the office workers coming in here for lunch. They even serve coffee.'

I can hardly believe my ears. Coffee! In the boozer?! How disgusting can you get? Still, I know what Sid is on about. A lot of the big houses around the common have been pulled down and in their place are posh blocks of flats catering for dynamic young executives. It is getting so the place is almost fashionable.

'You're shooting up the social scale a bit, aren't you, Sid?'

'No, not me, mate. I'm working class and proud of it.' This is a sure sign that Sidney is tucking away a bit of loot. When people are on the make they are always trying to act posher than they really are. Once they get a bit of cash and security they start telling everyone that success has not changed them and go around complaining about the price of brown ale.

'What are you doing then, Sid?'

Sid narrows his eyes into slits and tries to look like a cross between Charlie Clore and Paul Newman.

'These days you've got to move fast, Timmo. Things change so quickly you've got to be in and out. Grab the money while it's going and then get into something else. You can't sit back and make long term plans. The public are fickle.'

'But what exactly do you do, Sid?'

'Well, Timmo, in a nutshell. I see a new craze coming and I capitalise on it. Do you remember the hula hoop revival?'

'No, Sid.'

Sid looks disappointed. 'No, well maybe that's not a very good example. "Hulava good time." I think it was a bit subtle. A bit ahead of its time. By the way, you don't happen to know anyone who wants forty thousand hula hoops, do you? You could use them as cheap tyres for penny farthings, Or cut them open, seal one end and use them for storing marbles.'

'I'll keep my eyes open, Sid.' I will too. I can see all the signs that Sid's keen eye for a business disaster has not deserted him. How, I wonder, can he find the gelt to buy houses? He must still have some cash salted away from his Cromby Hotel days.

'But this latest one can't go wrong,' exults Sid. 'It's a sure fire winner. Nobody's really begun to tap the potential.'

'What is it?'

Sid looks round carefully as if the boozer might be crawling with industrial spies. 'Pogo sticks.'

'Pogo sticks!'

'Not so loud, you berk. I don't want to tell everybody.'

Sidney watches a couple leave the pub and I can see him wondering whether they are going to rush home and start dismantling the telly to make pogo sticks.

'You reckon they're going to catch on, do you?'

'With a bit of help from the right quarter. The art in this game is to get the merchandise before you start the craze. That way you get it cheaper.'

'I understand that, Sid. But it's a bit risky, isn't it? What about all those hula hoops?'

'I was unlucky there, Timmo. I didn't know all the little wrinkles. I've got a professional public relations adviser now.'

'What does he do?'

'He gets you into the papers without you having to pay for an advertisement. He's got lots of great ideas. We're going to have a pogo stick race round Trafalgar Square and an attempt on the world pogo stick high jump record outside Buckingham Palace. Imagine that! It will give the whole thing a sort of royal seal of approval. We're giving one to Ted Heath. He's athletic, isn't he?'

'Yes, but he can't use it on his yacht.'

'I dunno. When there's a calm and nothing much going on he might be glad to bounce up and down on the fo'c'sle. Think of the pictures we'll get. Everybody will want one.'

'What makes you think Ted Heath is going to accept your blooming pogo stick?'

'He won't have any alternative. We're going to send a frogman down to tie it on to the anchor.'

'I don't reckon he's going to like that, Sid.'

'I don't know about that. I just hope he accepts it in the spirit in which it is given.'

'That of wanting to make a load of bread, you mean?'

'Well, he's done all right, hasn't he? I don't see why he should object to chucking it about a bit. The Conservatives are champions of private enterprise, you know.'

Poor old Sid can be so naïve sometimes that it makes me want to weep.

'How does Rosie react to all this?' I ask.

'She's so wrapped up in her boutiques she doesn't know what I'm doing.'

'Boutiques?'

Sidney looks slightly deflated. 'Yeah. She's got two. Thinking of opening another one. She's got quite a flair for it.'

Good for Rosie. I wonder Mum wasn't rabbiting on about it. I suppose, being pre-women's lib, she reckons Sidney must have done everything.

'Must bring in a few bob.'

Sid looks downright uncomfortable. I can see where the money for his house is coming from.

'Yeah. It's handy of course. Gives her an interest, that's the main thing. Of course, it hasn't got any of the potential of my schemes. When one of these goes then, woosh! One's talking about tens of thousands.'

That's the trouble with Sid. He is always talking about tens of thousands. Never doing anything, just talking.

'I hope it all goes well for you both, Sid. That's a nice bit of stuff you've got there.'

Sid looks at his trendy whistle as if seeing it for the first time.

'Do you like it? I'm not sure, myself. It's one of Rosie's. To tell you the truth, I think I look a bit of a ponce in it.'

'I know what you mean,' I say. 'I think that bloke over there thinks so too.' In fact, the geezer in question is harmlessly reading his paper but he looks up when he sees Sid staring at him. Unbeknown to Sid I give him a little wave from behind his shoulder and the fellow waves back. Sid blushes scarlet and buries his mug in his glass.

'Blimey, you're right,' he says. 'The buggers are everywhere. I'm never going to wear this lot again.'

'Probably wise. I think that wrist chain is a symbol of The Gay Liberation Front, isn't it? Funny, I always think they should be called The Gay Liberation Behind.'

But Sidney is too busy tearing his bracelet off to listen to me.

'Let's get out of here.'

'Hang on a minute, Sid. Your friend might be over to buy you a drink in a minute.' But my desire to stay is not only occasioned by the embarrassment I am causing Sid. At the far end of the room are a couple of fair looking birds, one of whom definitely has eyes for me. They are both on the posh side but I reckon that they are not above the thought of romantic dalliance. Stands to reason, doesn't it? You don't get birds in a boozer unless they know their way around. Dinner time, too. Down at the office the old man is taking his corned beef sandwiches out of his brief case and they're out on the town. It's terrible, but it's life.

'Hang on a minute, Sid,' I say, grabbing him by the arm. 'I reckon we could be away there.'

Sid follows my eyes. 'Yeah. Brings back memories, doesn't it? This always has been a good place for pulling birds.'

For a moment I don't know what he is on about and then I remember my embarrassing experience when I was trying to show Sid how I could charm chicks and be a successful window cleaner. That seems a long time ago now.

'Where are you going?' I say to him as he strains for the door.

'I told you, I want to get out of this place.'

'Don't worry about him. He'll soon back off if he sees you prefer birds.'

'I've got to go shopping with Rosie this afternoon.'

'Go another time. She'll be all right without you.' It is depressing to hear Sid going on like this. I can remember when he went ape if he walked past the underwear counter at Marks and Sparks.

'I promised her.'

'Break it.'

'I can't.'

Fortunately my desire for Sid's presence diminishes strongly when the bird who showed signs of being able to resist me gets up and starts making as if she is about to leave.

'Right. Piss off then,' I tell Sid.

'Aren't you coming?'

'I think I'll stick around for a few minutes.'

'Don't you want to see Rosie?'

'Very much, Sid. But she is my sister. Use a bit of common. I haven't exactly been fêted with crumpet over the last three months. Just to see a bird is a new sensation.'

Sid shakes his head. 'I'd have thought that gang bang at the nick would have done you for three years. I don't know. In front of your own Mum and Dad, too.'

'It wasn't my fault, Sid. I was stoned, wasn't I? We all were. It could have happened to anyone.'

'Yeah. But when that bird climbed on the table—'

'I've told you before, Sid. I don't remember anything about it.'

My bird has got up now and looks as if she is about to follow her mate out of the pub. She gives me a real 'come and get it' look and goes into the ladies.

'That bloke is smiling at you again,' I lie.

'Right. I'm off,' says Sid, hurriedly. 'You're not coming, then?'

'No, I'll find my own way back. Give Dad a heart attack by telling him I've gone down the Labour.'

Sid pushes off and I take a quick butchers at myself in the mirror above the bar. My hair is a bit on the short side and I certainly have lost a lot of weight. Lean and hungry – very hungry. What am I going to say to the bird? A lot depends on whether I can catch her eye when she comes out of the khasi. If we have got a nice little smile going, then it doesn't matter what I say. Hang on, here she comes.

The little darling slips out of the toilet and without taking my eyes off her I coolly raise the water jug to my lips and take a sip from it. I realise my mistake when the spout collides with my cake-hole. Typical, isn't it? Bleeding Cary Grant never has my luck. The bird does a double take and before I can get back on track some other geezer wanders over and starts chatting her up. Together they walk to the door and in the space of a few cruel seconds my plans seem doomed to failure. I am so distressed that I take a giant swig from the water jug when meaning to knock back my beer.

'It tastes stronger than the piss you serve,' I say to the barman who is giving me an old-fashioned look, and move swiftly out of the boozer. All is not lost because my bird has separated from the bloke she was with and is walking towards a sports car. An M.G.B., no less. Can't be bad, can it? Only the best is good enough for Lea. Now what am I going to say to her? For a moment I cannot think of anything and then a giant wave of inspiration drenches me.

'Excuse me,' I say, belting to her side as her hand collides with the door handle. 'I wonder if you could help me?'

She gazes into my face and I am conscious that she must have been away on holiday or under a sunray lamp. There are little flecks of white at the corner of her eyes.

'What do you want?'

'My mate has just gone off without his keys. I meant to

give them back to him and I forgot. Do you think you could catch him up? He's only been gone a couple of minutes.'

'Won't he come back when he finds he hasn't got them?'

'He's going to Brighton, you see.'

'Oh, dear. Well, you'd better get in, hadn't you?' She slips inside the car and stretches across to open the door and – by the cringe! I darn near cream my jeans. The mixture of tit and exposed thigh is powerful stuff to a man in my position.

'Which way would he have gone?'

'Across the common, I reckon.' The M.G.B. rips away leaving behind a small smear of tyre rubber and I am thrown back into my bucket seat.

'Do you live around here?' asks my companion.

'All my life!' I say, trying to sound proud rather than defensive.

'We've only just moved in. We used to have a flat in Surbiton but it was a bit far out. Do I turn right here?'

'Left,' I say. I am feeling a bit short on words because we have pulled up at some traffic lights and Sidney is in the car beside us.

'Tell me when you see any sign of him,' says my unsuspecting friend.

'I will.' I lean across behind her and give Sid a friendly wave. He does not say anything but just watches, open-mouthed, as our car roars away. It is a very satisfying moment and one that I know I am going to cherish in the long winter nights to come.

'Do you think we've come the right way?'

'I think we may have lost him,' I say, trying to sound really broken up about it.

'Do you want me to take you back to The Highwayman in case he's gone back there?'

'Er–yes.' I should sound more enthusiastic but I am not eager to say goodbye to the lady so soon. 'Sure it's not taking you out of your way too much?'

'Oh, no. If he's not there you can come back to the flat and phone Brighton.'

'Brighton?'

'You said that was where he was going. Have you got the number?'

'Oh, yes.' I pull myself together. If it means getting into the bird's flat, of course I have the number.

'I suppose I can trust you, can I?'

Whenever a bird says that you can reckon that you are in like Flynn. What she is really saying is: 'Please make it perfectly clear that I can't trust you so that I know I'm not wasting my time with some goody-goody creep.'

'Worried about the ash-trays, are you?' I say, giving her the chance to spell it out.

'Not only that. You read some very disconcerting things in the papers. A girl isn't safe these days.'

Not if she wears no bra and a nylon blouse through which you could read the small print on a hire purchase agreement. Talk about man-made fibres, more like man-mad, if you ask me. And her perfume doesn't exactly act as a repellent either.

'You're safe with me,' I leer, delivering the famous Lea slow burn with a couple of ounces of nostril quiver chucked in at no extra charge.

'What's your name?'

'Timothy Lea. What's yours?'

'Elspeth Jones. But my friends call me Elly.'

'Very unusual name, Elspeth.'

'I hate it. My mother got it out of a romantic novel she was reading when I was born.'

'My Mum was like that with Timothy. She reckoned it was very genteel – I used to get the mickey taken out of me something dreadful at school.'

'Children can be very unkind, can't they?' says Mrs Jones, sympathetically. All the omens bode well for a nooky fest, the more so when The Highwayman hoves in sight without Sidney's ugly mug decorating the front of it. There is no reason why he should be there but with Sidney you never know. He can turn up with all the unwelcome inevitability of brewer's droop on your wedding night.

'His car isn't here,' I say, trying to sound disappointed. 'Oh, dear.'

'What a shame.' Mrs Jones is a good actress too. 'Well, you can use my phone if you want to.'

'If you're sure it's not too much trouble.' We look into each other's eyes for a couple of naughty moments and I can feel Percy stirring like a hibernating rock python that has just felt the first shaft of spring sunshine fall across its resting place after a long hard winter. Putting it another way, I reckon I am going to be up her faster than a rat up a drain pipe.

'It's not far.' Mrs Jones puts her foot down and the edges of my seat nearly touch in front of me. I wonder if she always drives like this. Probably suffering from an attack of Lea-lust. Who can blame her? My confinement in the clink must have ushered in a period of strain for quite a few birds.

The Jones pad is very much what I might have expected. Fill it with water and you would have the world's largest aquarium. I have nothing against glass but my fondness for it does not extend much beyond windows. I do not want the whole world gawping at me every time I scratch my action man kit.

'Nice place you've got here,' I say, looking at the spot where her legs meet. Mrs Jones pulls her skirt in the direction of her knees and noses her vehicle on to its slab of concrete.

'I think it's going to go up,' she says. I assume she is talking about the value of the flat, but she might just be a mind reader.

'How many girls do you share this with?' It is obvious that she is married but all birds are flattered if you think they are just out of blue serge knickers.

'I'm an old married woman,' she says. 'Three years.'

'Three years? Good heavens you hardly look past the age of consent.'

I have no idea what this is – probably about ten nowadays – but Mrs J. gets my drift.

'I don't know whether you mean that, but you've no idea how nice it is to receive a compliment again. I'd almost forgotten what it was like.'

'Surely your husband tells you you're attractive?'

'Yes, but it's not the same coming from him, is it?'

Sorry about that fellows, but once you have signed up with a bird you are on a hiding to nothing. If you don't tell her she is beautiful she will say that she might as well be dead because you never take any notice of her. Tell her that she is the most gorgeous bit of crumpet under the sun and she will say that your love is stifling her. There never is a right way with women.

'What does your husband do?' I ask as we trip through the foyer and discover that the lift is out of order. A toffee-nosed middle-aged woman is standing beside it and she looks at me as if she can read my mind and does not like some of the four-letter words she finds there.

'He works in an advertising agency.' The middle-aged hag looks even more disgusted.

'That must be very interesting.' We start walking up the stairs and Lady Shagnasty's eyes follow us like a couple of bloodshot private detectives. I turn round, screw up my face and throw her a big, wet kiss which shows her most of the inside of my lips. She turns away hurriedly.

'I don't know about interesting. They certainly get their money's worth out of him. I hardly see him. And when I do he's too exhausted to do anything but flop down in front of the telly. He brings home work at weekends and he's always cutting things out of the papers. It drives me mad. I'm right in the middle of something and then, suddenly, there's a great big hole.'

'I know the feeling,' I say sympathetically. 'My sister used to be like that. All the pop stars went, and the stuff on three pages behind.'

We have so much in common Mrs Jones and I. We must have been doomed for each other.

'Here we are.' Mrs Jones stops outside the door of Flat Number 69 and blushes. I do not know whether this is because the digits suggest something to her naughty little mind or because there is a red rose resting between the two yellow-top milk bottles.

'I have a very passionate milkman,' she says. 'He is always leaving me things.' I wonder why? I think to myself. My experiences as a window cleaner showed me that there are quite a few passionate customers about as well. Mrs Jones could well fit into that category. She strikes me as being quite a self-possessed lady and is quick to prove the point.

'One disadvantage of living in this place is the neighbours,' she says. 'They're always trying to organise your life for you. Maintenance committees for the lawn, sub-committees to decide what colour the flats should be painted. Nobody is allowed to be an individual.'

'I wouldn't like that,' I agree with her.

'I live my own life. I have my own set of values and I don't give a hang what anyone else thinks.'

'Very understandable.'

'I wouldn't have got married under any other conditions. I told Brian: "I demand to retain my freedom." If I want to take a lover, that's my affair. Would you like a cup of tea?'

'Er–yes. Yes thanks.' For some strange reason a faint feeling of nervousness comes over me. Mrs Jones is obviously one of those strong, passionate outspoken ladies who are filling the pubs with nervous men looking over their shoulders every time the door opens.

'Nobody in this place would understand that. They conform utterly. Did you see that old harridan by the lift?'

'You mean the vacuum cleaner?'

'No! The woman who was looking at us as if she reckoned we were going to be at it like knives the minute we got through the door.' She gazes at me and I swallow hard. It is bloody stupid but when she talks like that I feel quite embarrassed. I prefer to make the running while the bird traces 'Lea is fabulous' on a window steamed up by her own heavy breathing.

'Do you like milk and sugar?'

'Yes please. Two spoonfuls.'

'The telephone is over there.'

I say ta very much and look up the dialling code for Brighton.

'You can have something stronger if you like.' She says it like she reckons I need something stronger.

'No thanks. Tea is fine.'

'She's typical.'

'Typical?'

'The woman by the lift.'

'Oh yes.' Mrs Jones has sat down beside me and I should be feeling as chuffed as a bog with two pails. Damn it all! I haven't had a bit for three months. The bird is distinctly fanciable and hardly giving indications of having her legs bound together with Sellotape. What is the matter with me?

'Are you all right?'

'Fine thanks.'

'Have you found the dialling code?'

'Yes thanks.' I dial the code and the first numbers that come into my head.

'Good morning. Hang Chow Chinese Noodle Palace,' says a voice that sounds as if it comes from somewhere a good deal further east than Wapping Broad Steps.

'Hello, Sid. Is that you? Oh, no. It can't be can it?' Not unless Sid has got down by one of those speeded up films they show on the telly.

'Hang Chow Chin—' continues the voice patiently.

'Tell Sid I've got his keys, will you. I'll hang on to them

until I see him. I think there's a spare set in the top right-hand drawer of the desk.'

The voice at the other end of the line is beginning to get agitated.

'O.K. Yes, fine. All right. Yes, I will. 'Bye.' I ring off hurriedly. Mrs Jones smiles at me.

'So that's your business attended to?'

'Yes.' I stand up.

'Don't you want your cup of tea?'

'Oh, yes.' I sit down again.

'Relax.' Mrs Jones pats my wrist as if I am about to go into the dentist's surgery. That is exactly what it feels like, too. I try to think of something to say but nothing comes into my mind.

'I think this is the best time,' continues Mrs J. 'I saw the way you looked at me in The Highwayman. You don't have to be shy. If you want to make love to me, go right ahead.' She stretches out her long legs and leans back against the sofa.

'That's the kettle, isn't it?' I say, listening to the whistle and the sound of my heart beating.

'That's right.' Mrs J. shows no sign of moving and the noise is beginning to bore a hole through my lug-hole.

'Shall I make the tea?'

'Why not?' Mrs J. gives me one of her irritating smiles. What is beginning to alarm me is that Percy is showing no signs of interest whatsoever. In his present situation he should be hurling himself against the side of my Y-fronts like a maddened beast. But not a sausage. Not even a chipolata.

'Don't worry.' Mrs Jones stands up. 'I don't want to disturb the balance of the sexes. You sit there.'

She stalks towards the kitchen. I watch the see-saw motion of her big end and think dirty – really dirty. Still nothing happening in the action man department. This is serious. Maybe the clink has turned me into a latent homosexual –

so late it has only just caught up with me? No, that is impossible. But there must be something wrong with me. Perhaps, after three months without it—no, that doesn't seem likely either. There was a blooming great population boom after the war, wasn't there? I give Percy a worried nudge but he continues to show less enthusiasm than Arthur Rubinstein at a piano smashing contest.

'Do you want a piece of home-made cake?' Mrs J.'s voice comes from the kitchen.

'Yes please.' It occurs to me that it would be a good idea to subject Percy to a little first aid treatment. I can't just sit here with him sulking under my brushed denims. I make genteel 'I'm going for a piss' noises and scarper to the toilet. It is strange but the whole of the lower part of my body seems anaesthetised. It is not until I try shock treatment and plunge my spam ram under the cold tap that I feel anything. This is because I have plunged it under the hot tap by mistake.

If there was a flicker of life in the poor sod, this puts the kibosh on it. In its present condition you could lay my dick on a plate of roes on toast and not be able to spot the stranger.

I tuck my equipment away and prepare to face Mrs Jones. I don't like admitting it but in my heart of hearts I know that she is the reason why my get up and go has got up and gone. Suddenly, she seems so experienced and demanding. I need someone wilting and dependent. Some bird who reckons that I am fantastic and who can lay it on so thick that I want to make it true for her. Sitting on the sofa and picking up a lump of sugar with a pair of tongs Mrs Jones doesn't look as if she thinks I am fantastic. In fact she is looking disappointed. Disappointed? And I haven't even touched her yet.

'I think it better to be frank, don't you?' says Mrs J. indicating my char.

'Yes,' I say, shaking my head. She gives me an old-fashioned look and I try nodding instead.

'I need to be physically satisfied just like a man.'

'Very understandable.' I slop tea into the saucer and drop my spoon on the floor.

'Most women wouldn't admit that,' muses Mrs J.

'It's not easy, is it?' I mean to admit that you fancy a bit of the other if you are a bird. Mrs J. is swift to misunderstand me.

'No. I suppose I ask a lot from a man. I'm what you might call "demanding".'

'Really?' A mouthful of cake goes down the wrong way and I blurt crumbs all over the settee. 'You make a smashing cake.'

'Brian made it. He's a much better cook than I am.'

'Oh, well, it's very nice.' Now I look closely at Elspeth Jones I can see that she has a heavy down of hairs on her upper lip.

'I don't just mean size.' Percy is now making a field mouse look like King Kong. In fact I am not even certain he is still there.

'Stamina.' She practically spits the word into my lap. 'I once knew this fantastic Jamaican.' 'Don't tell me about him,' I screech silently. 'What a man. The most superb body I've ever seen. Great banks of gleaming black muscle. And he went on and on and—'

'I've heard they're very—'

'—on and on and on. I was a different person afterwards. That experience really showed me what sex could be like. It was never the same with Brian after that. I told him, of course.'

'You mean that it wasn't the same as—'

'Yes. It was a shock to him but I think he respected my integrity. He was seeing a psychoanalyst at the time, anyway.'

'Oh, well. That must have been a big help to him.'

Mrs Jones leans forward and takes the cup and saucer from my twitching fingers.

'Don't worry about the crumbs. Do you want to do it in here or in the bedroom?'

Now that I look into her face again she seems to be growing a beard. Oh, dear. I am really on the horn of a Dalai Lama. Half of me is saying 'you don't fancy it, so piss off' while the other half is saying 'don't be a berk, she's a lovely bit of stuff. Once you get her knicks off everything will be all right'. I know I will be pretty choked if I think about this afterwards and I have not had a crack at it. It is like refusing a bloke who is trying to give you bank notes.

'I don't mind stretching my legs,' I say weakly and haul myself to my feet. If I am going through with this I will have to break the hypnotic spell that my mind has cast over my hampton park. I will have to stop thinking about sex. If I can take the mental pressure off Percy then I may have a sporting chance of competing with black power.

'Are you interested in football, at all?' I ask as we go into the bedroom.

'I loathe it.' Mrs J. coolly unzips her dress and steps out of it. I notice that she is wearing a pair of those scarlet, transparent, embroidered panties with a frilly hem that have names like 'Casbah Madness'. I always wondered who wore them. Although their intention is clearly to turn the observer on, they have the opposite effect on me. There is something professional and rehearsed about them which makes me feel I am about to take part in a circus act. I would like there to be a spot of physical contact between us whilst we shred the threads but Mrs J. is stark bollock naked and lying on the counterpane before you can say Roger Carpenter. She has a fantastic body but it might be a waxwork for all the effect it is having on me.

'I support Chelsea, myself,' I tell her. 'We are the champions.'

'Come here and prove it,' says Mrs J. meaningfully.

Relax, I tell myself. Just imagine you are in one of those changing huts in the middle of Clapham Common. I sit down on the edge of the bed and start undoing my shoelaces. If I can persuade myself that I am in the process of changing for some commonplace sporting event I may be able to divert worried Percy from his current hang-ups and then suddenly spring Mrs J. on him when he is least expecting it. It's a proper carry on, isn't it? Seems ridiculous really.

'What are you whistling?' says a puzzled Mrs J.

' "Blue is the colour." '

'That's one of those ridiculous soccer songs, isn't it? Now what are you doing?'

'Just dribbling my sock over to the dressing table. Goal!!'

'Are you all right?' Mrs J. sounds worried. I wish she would belt up. How does she expect me to get it together if she keeps rabbiting?

'The ball's bobbing about on the edge of the penalty area. Osgood to Lea. Lea swings his right foot. Goal!! Wilson didn't move.' I raise my hands above my head in front of the wardrobe and catch a glimpse of Mrs J. watching me nervously from the bed. If I can recreate the atmosphere of an actual match, I may be able to break the spell. In my mind I emerge from the changing room and start running towards the pitch. It is drizzling and cold. Very cold. So cold in fact that my old man is beginning to shrivel up – no, you fool! That's not the effect I'm after. I start running around the room swinging my arms across my chest.

'Now what are you doing?'

'Warming up.'

'I can think of less selfish ways of doing it.'

'I'm going in goal.' I hurl myself across the bed and push one of the pillow cases on to the floor.

'Stop it!'

'Did you see that save? Fantastic. Here we go again. Wheeeeeh!'

'You're mad.'

'I'm football crazy.' I leap on to the bed and head the lightshade so that it swings into the middle of the room and a cloud of dust comes down.

'Stop it!' Mrs J.'s cool is clearly shattered and this cheers me up a bit. That worried look in her eyes makes me feel more like the male chauvinist pig I found I was when I read that article in one of the posh Sundays. Incidentally, if you fancy a spot of saucy reading I can thoroughly recommend the posh Sundays. They wrap it up a bit and you need a dictionary handy, but there is no doubt that you can get a lot of interesting sexual detail from the quality press – and it concerns a much higher class of person, too. Quite historical, some of it. I reckon I would have been far more interested in history at school if I'd known that they were having it away all the time.

I stand on Mrs J.'s leg, she screams and I lose my balance and sit down on her arm. She screams again.

'I'm sorry. Are you all right?'

'Are you all right? you mean. What's the matter with you?'

At last she touches me but it is only a restraining arm, no doubt intended to prevent me from getting my football boots on. I am a fool. I should never have got myself into this situation. I ought to have got out while I had the chance.

'Take the rest of your clothes off,' barks Mrs J. She might be saying 'Come in, number nine, your time's up,' for all the romantic feeling she can get into her voice.

I peel off my shirt and, without looking, ease down my Y-fronts. Maybe they are the trouble. All those tight jeans and athletes' briefs have suffocated the poor basket. Still, you can't wander about in bloomers, can you? Nobody would ever want to be exposed to the lustre of your cluster.

Mrs J. takes a deep breath and lies back expectantly. 'We've got three and a half hours,' she says.

'Three and a half hours!' Flipping heck! What does she

think I am? At this rate I'll be reading her nursery rhymes for the last three and a quarter. I look down at the faint moustache above her upper lip and wonder why I can suddenly smell Sloan's Linament.

'Why are you sniffing?'

'I thought I smelt something.'

'It must be my perfume. It's very unusual. I once had this Persian boyfriend. It used to drive him out of his mind. He used to say that he could catch a whiff of it at the bottom of the stairs. I always knew it was him when I heard the footsteps pounding along the corridor. I'd hardly have time to open the door before he'd burst through like some great animal and snatch me up into his arms.'

'Very strong blo—'

'And then he'd carry me through the flat and throw me down on the bed and—'

'It must have been very—'

'—on and on and on.'

Blimey! By the time she has stopped rabbiting Percy has got about as much backbone as a homeless whelk. I do wish she wouldn't go on like that – on and on and on.

'What's the matter?' she says.

'Nothing. I was just thinking.'

'What about?'

'Oh, nothing, really.'

'It must get rather boring?'

'I'm used to it.'

It's not vintage Noel Coward, is it? And Mrs Jones is not slow to realise that something is wrong. Nudging me with a shapely knocker, she raises herself on one elbow and sends her fingers down to reconnoitre the disaster area.

'Don't you find me attractive?' she says accusingly, having discovered less action than at an old age pensioners' jitterbugging contest.

'I don't know what it is,' I say weakly.

'I'm not certain that I do,' says Mrs J. unkindly, releasing her hold on my wilting willy. 'You're not queer, are you?'

Those must be, without doubt, the cruellest words my lugholes have ever cringed before. That I, Timothy Lea, Clapham's most exciting male animal, should be so accused and unable to stand up for himself. It does not bear thinking about, especially if – no, it can't be. Not me. Surely not. I mean—

'Are you? I don't mind. I've never been to bed with a queer.'

'Neither have I!' I say, indignantly. 'Do you mind? Every bloke who doesn't fancy you isn't a raving poufdah, you know.'

'If you're not queer, you're something very like it,' sniffs Mrs J. 'Coming in here playing football. Most men who come in here have got something better to do.'

'I'm not queer,' I repeat.

'Prove it.' Mrs J. leans across and kisses me hard on the mouth. It is nice of her to bother but I need gentler treatment.

'That was like a man's kiss!' I chide her.

'Ah! So you've been kissed by men?'

'No! Of course I haven't. I just imagined it would feel like that.'

'Do you think about it a lot?' Mrs J. sounds quite interested.

'I never bleeding think about it! I tell you: I'm not queer.' I swing my feet off the bed and grab my Y-fronts.

'Running away, are you?' mocks Mrs J. 'It just shows how wrong you can be about people. I thought you looked quite sexy when I saw you in The Highwayman.'

'I felt the same about you,' I say. 'I'm sorry but I think I'd better go.'

'Maybe you're not eating enough,' she says as I pull on my jeans. I look at her wriggling into her panties and for a moment I experience a twinge of lust. It is not worth pursuing, though. This bird and I are never going to be able to make it in a million years. I will probably never be able to make it again with any bird.

'I've got a book somewhere that might help you,' she says as we walk towards the door. ' "Sexual impotence, the beginning of the end." My husband found it very useful.'

'Thanks a lot, but I'm not much of a reader. I'll have to work it out for myself.'

Right up to the moment when the door closes behind me I have a feeling that some miracle is going to occur. That something will spark us off into a knicker-ripping assault on the carpet pile. But nothing does happen. I find myself standing outside the building and I still have all my clothes and the forty thousand million sperm cells I went in with. At least, that is what I used to carry. I probably have about half a dozen now and them barely able to travel the length of my tonk without a wheelchair. It is all very, very disturbing.

CHAPTER TWO

When I walk away from the flats my spirits are lower than the balls on a kneeling dachshund. I still cannot believe that it happened – or rather that it didn't happen. How could I, the answer to the secret love dreams of twenty-five million British birds, make such a hopeless cock up of it? 'Cock up'! I permit myself a wry smile. What a bleeding marvellous choice of words. And after three months Sellotape – or celibate, or whatever it is. I might as well knot myself. Twenty-two and on the way to the knacker's yard. It wasn't as if I was pissed or anything. I have absolutely no excuse. I look down at the smooth, unruckled front of my brushed denim jeans and feel like bursting into tears.

There is only one thing for it: get pissed. Fortunately, Mum has slipped me a few quid and the pubs are still open. I go into the nearest boozer and order a double scotch. I get in a couple more and then buy a half bottle to take on the common when the pub closes. The more I think about things the more depressed I get. Not just about sex but about my life as a whole – or as a hole, more like. The nick was pretty bad but I relish living at home less than being a chalet maid at an eskimo nudist camp. I have had half a dozen different careers and I would have made more cash if I had become a yak sexer and signed on for unemployment benefit. Nothing seems to go right for me. And one of the main reasons for that is bleeding Sidney. He is always messing me about. What I need is a complete change of scene. I must get away from the suffocating pressures of home life.

I turn my back on the couple who are practically having it away in the shelter in the under-sixes playground and consider what to do next. Two old birds wander past and one of them shakes her head as she looks at me. 'Terrible, isn't it?' she murmurs to her companion as they both stare at my half-empty bottle.

She is dead right, of course. Fifty years later I could still be sitting here, only with a bottle of meths. I must do something to change my aimless, self-indulgent life. Pausing only to swig down the rest of the scotch, I hurl the bottle into the nearest litter bin and immediately feel a better man. A new sense of purpose, that is what I need. Starting from next weekend I will begin watching 'Stars on Sunday'.

Right now, I see that there is a revival of 'Titty, Titty, Gang Bang' at The Roxy, Balham, and I might just be able to catch the main feature. I don't want to waste the whole afternoon.

But I never get to the The Roxy. The way to the cinema takes me past the Army Careers Information Office. Normally, it takes me past it bleeding fast, but today I am in a state fast approaching the pissed and I stop and have a butchers through the window. I should be warned when the bloke with sergeant's stripes and peaked cap nearly covering his tash leaps to his feet like a monkey seeing a banana walking past its cage.

My attention has been caught by a placard in the window showing a bloke dressed up in a white ski suit, with a fur hood, sub-machine gun and goggles. He is carrying – would you believe it? – a pair of skis. The bloke looks very like me, as do lots of people when you can only see the ends of their hooters, and releases in me a tidal wave of wish fulfilment. Looking at him I can see myself, completely on my tod, skimming up and down mountain peaks while some kid whistles the theme music from 'Shane' in the background – if he couldn't whistle that I would settle for '633 Squadron'.

'Good afternoon! Thinking about becoming a professional, are you?' The voice is brimming over with friendly enthusiasm and issues from the cake-hole of the sergeant who is now standing in the doorway.

'I was just looking,' I say, defensively.

'Look away, laddy. That's what it's all there for. You like skiing, do you?'

'I've never done any.'

The sergeant shakes his head sympathetically.

'It's a wonderful sport. You haven't lived 'til you've been on skis. And taught at the Army's expense, too. It doesn't seem credulous, does it?'

'You do that in Germany, do you?' I hear myself saying.

'Germany, Norway, Cyprus. In Cyprus you can snow ski in the morning and be water skiing in the afternoon. All that and twenty-nine pounds thirty-three p before you even get a stripe up. What a life for a young man, I only wish I had my time again.'

'Yeah.' I take another look at the bloke on skis. It would certainly be a lot different to Scraggs Lane, wouldn't it?

'It's changed out of all recognition since I first went in. No bull, choice of first class food. Lots of free time to follow up your own private interests. Like skiing, for instance.'

Of course, I can see it all. Check in your rifle about four o'clock and then up and down the ski runs until it's time for a mug of edelweiss and a spot of clog dancing. Must be the life, mustn't it? I don't know why I never thought of the Army before. Ooh, I do feel dizzy.

'Come in and sit down and I'll answer any questions you may have,' says the kindly sergeant. I follow him inside and he picks up the evening paper lying on his desk and throws it to one side. Funny that it should be open at the 'Sits. Vac.' section.

'Now, lad. What branch of the service were you thinking about? Infantry?'

'I hadn't really thought—'

'That would be the best for the skiing, wouldn't it? Build up the leg muscles nicely. There's a lot of famous regiments, you know. You a local boy, are you?'

I nod.

'How about the Light Division?'

'I can't even mend a fuse.'

'No, laddy.' The friendly sergeant grits his teeth for a fleeting second. 'I meant the Light Infantry or the Green Jackets. If we can make a decision today I can practically guarantee you the choice of any regiment you care to mention.'

'Are there any skiing regiments?'

The kindly sergeant shakes his head regretfully.

'No, laddy, I'm afraid not. But you could well find yourself being seconded to a Norwegian unit on a N.A.T.O. exercise. You know all about our obligations to N.A.T.O., don't you?'

'You mean the president of Yugoslavia?'

'No, lad. I meant – oh, it doesn't matter.' He reaches for a form. 'Now, let's see. You want to join the infantry and you want to ski. It's a question of how many years it's going to take to make you a Jean Claude Killer.'

Suddenly, things seem to be going a bit fast and I wish I hadn't knocked back that half-bottle of scotch. I don't feel a hundred per cent in control of the situation.

'It could be three or six or—'

'I was thinking more of—'

'If you spoke a bit of German it could make it easier with the skiing.'

'Yeah, well I think maybe I'd better—'

'Do you know what the German for "no" is, lad?'

'Nein,' I say, proudly.

'Nine? Very good, lad. Right, sign here.'

'You signed on for nine bleeding years?' says Sid. 'You must be round the twist.'

'I was conned,' I bleat. 'I didn't know what I was doing.'

'You seldom do, Timmo. But at least you don't let yourself in for a caper like this. Blimey! Nine years. You'll be out in time for the Clapham Olympics, won't you?'

'Make a man of him,' says Dad who has accepted the news

of my enlistment with something approaching rapture.

'What would you know about it?' says Sidney. 'The nearest you ever get to the Army is watching the Trooping of the Colour on the box.'

Dad does not take kindly to this slur. 'You don't know nothing about it, clever sticks. This family has got a tradition of service. My feet let me down but it didn't stop me doing my bit. You were hardly bleeding born then so you've got nothing to talk about.'

I don't know what Dad means when he rabbits about 'tradition of service'. I remember that Aunty Nora was in the W.R.A.C.s and rumoured to throw it about a bit but I think that was the sole Lea contribution to the war effort. The male members of the family collapsed the moment a stethoscope touched their chests.

'It doesn't matter, Dad,' I say wearily. 'By the time I've finished I'll have made up for every war the family missed since the Crusades.'

'I hope you like it, dear,' says Mum. 'You haven't stuck at anything else for very long, have you?'

Sidney snorts. 'He won't have any difficulty sticking at this. They'll see to that all right.'

'I don't see what made you do it, dear,' says Mum. 'You never talked about the Army before.'

'It was the skiing, Mum.'

'Skiing?'

'Don't sound surprised, Mum,' says Sid. 'Surely you noticed? You can hardly cross the road these days without a platoon of blokes on skis comes whizzing past. It's not surprising, is it? I mean, with all the mountains there are about here and the weather.'

'What are you on about?' says Mum.

'He's taking the piss, Mum,' I say bitterly. 'I just happened to mention the appeal of the outdoor life and how I hoped to get some skiing in.'

'It's like joining the French Foreign Legion because you

fancy dates,' says Sid. 'I tell you, he's stark, raving bonkers.'

'Shut your face, Big Mouth,' says Dad, springing to my defence for the first time in living memory. 'I know why he done it. He was trying to cleanse the blot from the family scrotum—'

'Escutcheon, Dad.'

'That as well. Like that bloke in that book by James Mason – wonderful talent that man, he was blooming magnificent as Rommel. Of course, you wouldn't know anything about Rommel, would you, skiver?'

'Get on with it, you old rat bag.'

'—The Four Feathers, that was the name of it. This fellow had done wrong so he went out to fight the wogs and make up for it. Just like our Timmy, see? He landed in the nick, didn't he? Now he's going to make it up. Send a few quid home to his old Mum and Dad who've stood by him through thick and thin.'

Sidney nods his nut up and down. 'I see it all, now. You put the idea in his head, did you? The only bleeding job he can hold down is one he won't get fired from. Fired at, of course, but that's—'

'Oh, belt up, all of you!' I shout, feeling something snap inside me. 'I signed on because I was conned and pissed. None of you had anything to do with it, except that I've had a basin full of the lot of you and I reckon anywhere would be an improvement on this place.'

My words are not slow to make an impression on my father. 'That's nice, isn't it? Blooming nice. After all we've done for him, too. Right, that's it. I'm washing my hands of him after that.'

'You want to wash your hands after a few more things,' I tell the miserable old git. 'They don't put those notices up for fun, you know.'

Dad turns scarlet. 'You foul-mouthed little bleeder. How dare you talk to me like that. We welcome you back home after you've dragged the family name in the dust and that's all the thanks we get.'

'You're right, Dad,' chips in Sid. 'After all you've done for him, too. It's diabolical how he can talk like that to his own flesh and blood.'

'You can shut your mouth, too,' says Dad, who to do him justice, has no favourite when it comes to a verbal punch-up. 'If I had any of your blood in my veins I'd have a transfusion tomorrow.'

'You'd never find anything that would stick inside your rotten body,' says Sid. 'It would run back up the tube and form a clot at the mouth of the bottle.'

'Don't let's have any unpleasantness,' says Mum, who is no sister to lightning when it comes to stamping out agro at source. 'Let's give Timmy a few happy memories of family life to take with him.'

She dabs at a tear and shakes her head. 'I don't know what we've done to deserve his hatred. We've never had a lot to give but—' I can see that we're in for a right lughole bashing so I step in swiftly.

'I'm sorry, Mum,' I say. 'I didn't mean what I said. I just thought it would be better for everybody if I had a change of scene. I always remember how Sid's Uncle Fred used to say that the Army made a man of you. It was just before the Military Police came and took him away.'

'There was still no cause for you to be so outspoken,' sniffs Mum.

'Yeah. I remember Uncle Fred,' says Sid. 'He always used to say that if he had his time again he'd do the same thing – and he ended up doing it. Poor bastard, it nearly killed him.' He looks me up and down and I know what he is thinking.

'Nine bleeding years. I still can't properly believe it. When are you leaving us, Timmo?'

'I'm waiting for a movement order at the moment.'

'Blimey. It won't seem the same without him, will it? It's

a shame really because I was going to let you in on my pogo stick operation.'

That is the first time that I can see a benefit from going in the Army since I sobered up.

A buff envelope arrives the next morning and encloses a travel warrant to a place called Westery which is the home of the First Battalion of the Royal Loamshires. Nobody knows where Westery is but we eventually discover it on the Welsh border.

'Bleeding good choice for someone who comes from London,' says Sidney. 'Don't forget to take your wellington boots with you.'

'Why? Does it rain a lot?'

'Not only that, Timmo. You can stand the sheep's legs in them. They don't have a lot of girls up there, you know.' Sidney can be very coarse sometimes.

I had wondered if Mum and Dad might organise some entertainment to celebrate my last night in the old homestead but the answer is short and typical: no. I can't even think of a bird who would want to see me, especially in my present condition. I have not had a spot of in and out for nearly four months now and Percy hangs about like a neutered tom that has just had its worm powders. I have seen more life in a bowl of sodden sugar puffs.

The next morning, Mum gives me a hug, Dad grunts and I am on my way to the station. It occurs to me as I approach the platform that the friendly sergeant and his pals have managed to rustle up a few more prospective world class skiers. A number of depressed-looking individuals are thumbing through the acres of tit displayed on the paperback section of the bookstall without finding much to bring a smile to their preoccupied mugs. I join them and select a volume entitled *John Adam in Eden*, which I hope will do something to recharge my jaded appetite. We walk towards the train and there is a feeling of corporate discomfort such as I would imagine exists in the queue outside a

V.D. clinic. Everybody wondering how they got themselves into this mess and wishing that they did not have to be seen with such a bunch of berks.

Fortunately there are other sights more worthy of the attention of my beady mince pies. One tiny chick with open, innocent eyes and a hooter of doll-like delicacy is staggering along with a heavy suitcase brushing against the hem of her tweed suit. Her dainty rosebud lips are pursed with effort and I practically rupture myself to get to her side. Unfortunately there are others present with exactly the same thought in mind and I finish a bad third.

'Thank you so much,' says the bird and she looks at the bloke carrying her case like he has just discovered a new form of penicillin. That is the kind of bird I like. Sweet, gentle and grateful. She wouldn't be telling you to lag your old man before you gave her one. I reluctantly tear my eyes away from her and concentrate on the bint who has come abreast of me. And when I say 'come abreast' I mean come abreast. Talk about Knockerama Holiday. Her tits make Jane Russell look like the before part of a bust developer ad. Her make-up is put on so thick that it seems to stand away from her mug like a badly registered colour photograph and her hair looks as if you only have to touch it for the whole lot to disintegrate into a pile of crinkly ash. Not that I would climb over her to get to Harold Wilson. The way she slaps the make-up on shows a willingness to please that never fails to win my gratitude. It is a little bit clumsy, too, and that helps me to experience that necessary feeling of superiority. She puts down her suitcase and smiles at me.

'Could you?' she says. That is a difficult question to answer at the present time but I think she is talking about carrying her suitcase.

'I'd be pleased to,' I say, nearly snatching the handle out of the top of the case in my enthusiasm.

'Are you enlisting?'

'Yeah.'

'Capital. I'm certain to see you later. You see, I look after the eunuch library.'

I can't see what eunuchs want with their own library but then I suppose they probably have more time to read than other blokes. I don't like the way she reckons me as a prospective customer, though. Maybe my inability to get it up is beginning to show. And just when I was feeling a bit more like my old self, too.

'Very interesting,' I say.

'Oh. Do you like books? How super.' She has a very posh voice, this bird and I reckon she would be the perfect playmate for the purple-headed bed snake if given the right kind of encouragement.

'I try to keep abreast,' I say. 'But I don't read enough. I never seem able to find the time.'

'You're going to be pretty busy in the next few weeks,' she says sympathetically. 'After that I hope you'll be able to make use of my facilities.'

'I hope so,' I say, with a feeling as I grab another eyeful of her breastworks. She goes into a first class compartment and I pad behind her and bung her suitcase on the rack.

'Thank you so much,' she trills. 'Miss Rosemurch. *A bientôt.*'

'Goodbye, Miss Bientot,' I say, realising that she is sending me back to the second class where I belong. 'I hope we meet again.'

It is funny because you would never think she was French to look at her. Probably her old man was a frog and slipped her Mum a quick one on a day trip to Bolougne. And fancy getting lumbered with a monicker like Rosemurch. Some parents have no feelings, do they?

I start trudging down the corridor and who should catch my eye, four compartments down, but the demure looking little bird I took a shine to earlier. She is on her own and opening a copy of one of those women's magazines which make birds dissatisfied with their lot – or little, as they soon think of it. '500 ways to make your man give you better orgasms' shouts one of the headlines on the cover. By the cringe, she can't be all that innocent if she is reading that stuff. I hope she does not take it too seriously.

With practised smoothness I slide back the door and nonchalantly toss my Chelsea F.C. canvas bag onto the rack. Having given her a taste of gracious living I then chuck myself into a seat and lean back to see that my zipper has popped open. A quick glance shows me that Miss Mouse is tucked away behind her magazine, so averting my eyes from the headline that reads 'Sex maniacs. How to defend yourself', I dart my hand down to repair the damage. No sooner have my fingers closed round the zip than the bird drops her magazine and looks me straight in the thighs. It is not a sight that occupies her attention for long. Springing to her feet she crosses to the windows facing the corridor and pulls down the blinds.

'Don't waste it,' she says.

What is she on about? And why has she drawn the blinds? I could understand her thinking that I might have been about to indulge in a spot of cock-robbing but, surely, most birds would reach for the communication cord when on the point of being threatened with a rampant nasty.

'I know what it's like,' she says. 'I used to do it all the time and I felt so ashamed. It became so I never thought about the real thing. I lived in a world of glossy, celluloid fantasies. And the more I did it the more unhappy and bitter I became. I wanted to give, you see, and to give only to oneself is utterly selfish and frustrating.'

'I was trying to—'

The lady holds up her hand.

'I know. It's difficult to talk about it, isn't it? You don't have to try and explain. I find men doing it in front of me all the time.'

'I wasn't—'

'Of course not. Don't be ashamed. At least you had the courage to do it in the open. I used to go down to the loo when I'd seen someone attractive.'

The train gives a jerk and pulls away from the platform and I watch the faces of a handful of parents who have come to wave goodbye to their offspring. One or two of the women are crying. Probably with relief. Opposite, the bird is staring at me intently.

'Would you run away if I did it to you? I tried it once with a man. I reached out to touch him and he zipped himself up so fast that I think he did himself an injury.'

I should think so too. Poor bloke must have had a fit. Like going to one of those German bars and finding that the bird you are dancing with plays inside right for Borussia Dortmund. Fancy her not realising that. Women can be very insensitive sometimes.

'Do what to me?' I say, reckoning that she knows what she is doing and I might as well leave her to get on with it.

'Show myself to you.'

And, so help me, she pulls up her skirt and starts wriggling out of her knicks. Blimey, it's amazing, isn't it? You don't even see things like that on the telly.

'Is that what you want to see?'

Well, it's certainly better than 'Crossroads'. Usually, it is the fat old bags who sit down opposite you with their legs apart. Talk about an awful eyeful. Every time I see a horsehair sofa with a slit in the side of it I blush. My new friend is a much more attractive proposition. And so helpful too.

'Now you can show yourself to me,' she says. 'Isn't it better with us doing it together?'

'Come over here,' I say. 'I think I'd find it easier with you close to me.'

'I know what you mean. It's a bit frightening out in the open, isn't?' She scampers over to my side and her mouselike mits grab hold of the entrance to Percy's stable. Man's best friend is beginning to respond in the manner of a bucking bronco held in check until the moment of its appearance in the rodeo ring. The zip goes down and – Shazam!! It's SUPERTONK! Suddenly the little lady has her hands full and my own ferret fingers make tracks for fursville. A kiss seems not inappropriate at this moment and our mouths complete the circuit which is pumping currents of thigh-trembling lust through our unresisting bodies. After my months of self-deprivation and self-doubt, my sense of relief is only matched by my desire to make sure that Percy has, in all respects, returned to his former state of rude good health. Allowing myself a guttural grunt which I hope will convey my feelings more eloquently than words, I pull my new friend on to the floor and wriggle my jeans down to knee level with a speed that threatens to start a fire between my thighs.

'It's better like this, isn't it?' she says unnecessarily and I disappear into her body like a deep sea diver sliding into a vat of treacle. Ardent fans will know that I am no stranger to mobile nooky and by now the British Rail symbol automatically makes me think of opening time – and I don't mean pubs. Miss Mouse grips Percy like a velvet vice and her head is whipping from side to side fit to roll off and disappear under one of the seats.

'You're saved! You're saved!' she gasps and I reckon she is not far from the truth. Another few weeks without oggins and who knows what would have happened? Nothing probably, but on a permanent basis—? It makes me think that there is definitely something to recommend the 'Belt up and cop this lot!' technique which my gentle nature has always rejected as being a bit on the coarse side. Maybe I should be more aggressive. After all, 'a hand up your bird is worth two on her bush' as the poet puts it. You can miss a lot by hanging about for the 'welcome aboard' signal.

Such thoughts are bombarding my tiny mind while I slip my body into overdrive and whack my gentle little friend round the threadbare carpet pile. It is a lot more fun than peeling five tons of potatoes but it does not serve to protect me from an increasingly painful realisation. One of the reasons why I was able to come to terms with my ill-considered decision to join the Army was that my inability to indulge in hanky pancreas meant that a complete change of scene was acceptable if not actually desirable. Now that Percy is banging away like a good 'un again, who needs H.M. Forces? I wonder if they would mind if I said it was all a mistake and that I had changed my mind? Something deep inside me tells me that the answer to that is probably yes.

Something deep inside my new friend is now telling me that it wishes to discharge its responsibilities and with the knowledge that ticket collectors have been known to interrupt such nooky carnivals as we are engaged upon, I enter into a short period of homage to the steam engine followed by sending Percy on an instant slimming course.

'O-o-o-o-o-h,' says the lady – or it might have been 'A-a-a-a-rgh' I can't really remember. 'That was lovely. Is that the first time you've done it with a girl?'

I am not certain that I find that very flattering so I refrain from comment and breathe heavily.

'Is it?' she persists, ruffling the hair behind my ears. I wish she would not do that. After I have shot my load I do not like birds fiddling about with me. Once PERCY has become Percy again I always feel a little sad. My sensitive nature, I suppose.

'Not quite,' I say.

'I know,' she says, pulling me even closer to her. 'You raped somebody, didn't you? That was how it happened with me. I hated it at first but then I realised that Henry was even more terrified than I was.'

'You knew him, did you?' I ask, beginning to get interested.

'Not at the time. It happened in an empty railway compartment – of course, it wasn't completely empty, I was there.'

'Yes,' I say patiently.

'I think when you started—'

'Yes.' I say hurriedly.

'It reminded me of it all.' The bird looks almost starry eyed.

'I screamed and struggled and all that kind of thing and then, when it was over, we started talking. He was terribly upset about what he'd done and I suddenly realised that he was very like me. Obviously sexy but very unsure of himself. He had done what I didn't have the courage to do. That was the only difference. It was before Women's Lib., you see.'

'Naturally.' I mean, since Women's Lib. blokes have been getting raped all over the place, haven't they? It is becoming so you hardly dare nip out for a packet of fags without changing your underpants. I return my eyes respectfully to Miss Mouse. What full, rich lives some people lead.

'We talked some more and then we did it again. This time I really enjoyed it. I think that being raped is a very good way to lose your virginity. You're so busy struggling that you don't notice the pain.'

'Did you ever see the bloke again?'

'Oh, yes. We got engaged eventually. It didn't work out, though. We could never recapture the first fine careless rapture.'

'Or rupture,' I say wittily.

My lady friend blinks down at me uncomprehendingly. I don't think she has much of a sense of humour.

'But the second time when we did it, it was gorgeous.' Her hand disappears between my legs like it is patting a pet pekinese and she gazes into my mince pies dreamily. I may be wrong but I think she has other things on her mind besides the world potato shortage. Percy certainly thinks so and begins to lumber towards the ceiling.

'Oh good. He wants to play again,' says my friend and she dives on to my mouth like the last one to get there is a cissy. Good sense demands that I shrug her contemptuously aside and go back to counting the telegraph poles, but it is not in my heart and Y-fronts to do so. After my last pubic appearance I am anxious to get rid of all Percy's hang-ups – or, more properly, hang-downs – and I dunk myself in her doughnut before you can say bun cap.

My natural reservoir of good taste makes me refrain from describing the action in detail and I will only say that when the ticket collector eventually arrives, there are beads of sweat running down the insides of the windows. Fortunately, I am fully clothed by then and in a fit state to receive visitors. Miss Mouse – or Amanda Nasty as I now know her – has nipped off to the toilet so I am turfed out of the compartment without having the chance to say goodbye to her. I hang about outside the nearest khasi but after about twenty minutes a fat geezer comes out who looks in a worse state than I am. When I stick my head round the door I get a good idea why.

I go back to the compartment but there is no one there so I find a seat in second class, intending to come back later. In fact, I end up having a kip which lasts until I hear someone belting out 'Westery!' at the top of his voice. I only just have time to grab my bag and dive off the train before it starts moving again.

The station we are at looks pretty rustic by main line standards and I imagine that the train only stops there by appointment to drop off poor berks like me who have signed their lives away. Why was I in such a bleeding hurry to get off? It took them long enough to catch up with Uncle Fred. I look around and there, amongst all the blokes standing about like spare pricks at a whore's wedding, is my little lady friend looking as if butter would not melt between the cheeks of her arse. I am on the point of stepping forward to congratulate her on not being separated from me when, once again, somebody gets there first.

This time it is a tall military gentleman wearing a trench coat and carrying a leather baton. He has a peaked cap and a crown on his shoulder. His face is lined and the pinky bits that run through his eyes seem to carry on into his nose and cheeks. He looks tired and narked and glances at the new recruits like they arrived in the cleats of one of his boots. One look at his miserable mush tells me that he is never going to be asked to host a telly programme for kiddies.

'Daddy.' The rapist's friend is addressing him and actually giving him a hug.

'Pull yourself together, Amanda. Not in front of the men.' Amanda's Daddy brushes her aside like she has just dropped on to his shoulder from a bunch of bananas and I shrink into the shadows. The major does not look the kind of geezer who would take kindly to the news that you had been introducing your spam ram to his daughter's nether regions.

'Don't be an old cross patch, Daddy.'

Daddy ignores his little girl and looks round as if searching for something. I turn away but—

'Hey you! Don't skulk, man. Are you for the Loamshires?' There is no doubt about who is being addressed.

'Yes. Yessir.'

'Well, put my daughter's bag in the car and get a move one. You're in the Army now, remember.'

Amanda's eyes open wide as she sees me but there is no opportunity for conversation as I stagger towards the battered Alvis.

'I'm sorry—' I begin, but Amanda holds a finger up to her lips. 'Don't talk now. Daddy is in one of his moods. I expect I'll see you at the camp.'

I hate to have to agree with her but there seems little immediate chance of us going on a package tour to Tunisia together.

'Right. Now double over to the rest of your intake.' I have hardly had time to wish I had closed the boot on the Major's fingers than he is rabbiting at me again. 'Come on, move.'

I have half a mind to tell him to piss off – and I reckon to get stuck with this lot I must have half a mind, period. Feeling a right berk in front of Amanda I start making tracks for the crowd of blokes I can see being herded into lorries.

A man with a face like a leaking hot water bottle and Sergeant's stripes on his arms is standing with his hands on his hips and hawking up words like they have been stuck half way down his throat. 'Where the hell do you think you've been?' he squeals. 'Sightseeing? Do you reckon this is a bleeding charabanc trip? Get inside you horrible little man. You're wasting the Army's valuable time and money.'

'I was helping—'

'Don't argue with me, lad.' The sergeant leans forward so I get the chance to find out that he must clean his teeth with a lavatory brush. 'Don't start throwing your weight around with me or I'll have you in the guard-room so fast your feet won't touch the ground.' He pauses for a moment, waiting for me to mutiny, and then continues. 'What's your name?'

'Timothy Lea. What's yours?'

'Watchit!!'

'What's your first name?' I know I am asking for trouble but he is a real Dad-class prick, this fellow. In fact, if they took a nostril each, I don't know which of them would get up my bracket furthest.

'Getinthattruck!'

'He's beautiful when he's mad, isn't he?' I say as I scramble over the side of the truck and my bag whistles over my head to bash against the back of the driver's cab.

Most of the blokes in the truck are a bit younger than me and none of them have their skis with them. They look about as miserable as I feel and more inclined to show it.

'It's not what I expected,' says a thin bloke with one of the saddest faces I have ever seen not being worn by a bloodhound.

'What do you mean? We haven't been anywhere yet.'

'I thought they'd stopped all the shouting and carrying on like that.'

'Maybe they've just stopped shouting about it.'

'You want to look out for that fellow. He took a dislike to you.' The thin bloke speaks very slowly and has some kind of northern accent which reminds me of when I was flogging floor cleaners. Those were the days. When will I realise when I am well off? Of course, there was Sidney, but even he doesn't seem so bad now. Better the devil you know and all that cobblers.

'Don't worry about him,' I say. 'He's all mouth. He'll calm down in a few days.' I know all about it because I have seen all those old war films on the telly, haven't I? Give it a week and Sergeant Watchit will be sitting on the end of your bed handing round bits of chocolate.

I look over the tailboard and there is the Alvis with Major Nasty waiting impatiently to pass – only the lorry, I think, but from the expression on his face, you can't be sure. He toots angrily and Amanda gives a little wave as they roar past.

'Do you know her?' says the bloke beside me, impressed.

'I picked her up on the train,' I say nonchalantly.

'Blooming heck! You didn't waste any time.' The voice hits exactly the note of admiration I am seeking.

'Life's too short, isn't it?' I look down and there is Miss A. Bientot in one of those little Italian numbers.

'Cor! Cop a load of the knockers on that one!' says my companion. Everyone cranes forward and the truck threatens to stand on its arse. Miss Bientot throws me a little wave and overtakes gratefully.

'Was she waving at you?'

'I bumped into her on the train.'

'Blimey. I wouldn't mind bumping into her and all. I don't know what you're doing in this lot, mate. If I could pull birds like that I'd still be in civvy street.'

The words sink into me like a knife but I give the speaker

my throw-away smile which many people think I should have thrown away years ago.

'You can get fed up with birds, can't you?' None of the faces I can see around me seem inclined to agree so I accept a cigarette and smoke in silence. It is only just beginning to dawn on me that I am actually in the Army. Like a bloke hearing the cell door shut behind him or the vicar say 'I now declare you husband and strife'.

The countryside we are driving through has a lot of high hedges so it is difficult to see what else it has got. I do catch a glimpse of mountains, though, and one of the blokes says that they are in Wales. Bleeding exotic, isn't it? I have only been in the Army a few hours and I am practically posted abroad.

'Fancy a leek, mate?' says one joker.

'Up your arse,' says a thick-set character with one eyebrow that stretches across his forehead and has more hair on it than he has on the rest of his head. I have heard him speak about half a dozen times and this is the only phrase he seems capable of uttering. The delivery does not change much either. A few more like him about and Scraggs Lane will seem like the London School of Economics.

I get a view of row upon row of huts set amongst trees and the lorry swings off the road and enters the camp. A weighted pole drops into place behind us and the road out of the camp is blocked. Nine years! Whatever made me do it?

CHAPTER THREE

'Right! Let's have you! Three ranks in front of me. Move! Asyouwere!!! Move!! Asyouwere!!! You're like a bunch of pregnant fairies.'

'If I was I'd have a bleeding miscarriage,' pants the bloke struggling beside me as we stumble backwards and forwards bashing each other with our suitcases.

The minute the tailboard comes down Sergeant Watchit's voice starts battering our lugholes and it does not let up for three minutes by which time we are standing in an equal number of untidy lines. This manoeuvre accomplished without loss of life the sergeant permits himself a theatrical silence – and sweeps his eyes up and down our ranks as if he can barely stomach what he can see.

'Right, you horrible shower,' he continues. 'My name is Sergeant Lake and I'm going to be your guide, philosopher and fiend for the next fourteen weeks. Who said that??!!'

Everybody looks at me so I turn round and stare accusingly at the bloke behind.

'I've warned you once. Don't let's have any smart-Alecks. I can't abide clever dicks.'

'The one that made him wasn't very clever, was it?' says my companion.

'Silence! I'm the only one who opens his mouth when I'm talking. When I read your names, fall out and leave your cases in the appropriate barrack room, A, B or C. They're clearly marked so the meanest intelligence should have no difficulty finding out where he lives. After you've done that, double out here and Corporal Martin will take you to draw kit.'

'Ooh! Goody, goody! Art classes already!'

'Right. I warned you. You're on a charge. Let that be a warning to the rest of you. What's your name?'

'What's a charge, Sergeant?'

'Don't ask me questions! You'll find out when you come up in front of your Company Commander. What's your name?'

'Bell, Sergeant. But I don't—'

'Shurrup!! When you've drawn your kit you'll have something to eat and be back here by eighteen hundred hours. Do you understand?'

'When's eighteen hundred hours, Sergeant?' says the mournful looking cove.

'God almighty! Haven't you heard of the twenty-four-hour clock?'

'Ours has only got twelve hours on it.' The voice sounds like 'Worried, Tooting'.

'Are you trying to take the piss?'

'No, Sergeant.'

'Six o'clock. When you've been down to the cookho— I mean, the Junior Ranks Restaurant, back here! Now, when I give the order: "fall out", turn smartly to the right, pause, two, three, and double away into your barrack room. Are you ready? Right. Platoon. F-a-a-a- Wait for it!! Platoon. F-a-a-a-a-all Owt! I said right, you stupid twerp!'

We hit the inside of the barrack room like it is full of gold nuggets and we have been given empty bags and told to help ourselves.

I don't know where they took the pictures in the Army Careers Information Office but it might have been Buckingham Palace compared to this place. Two rows of iron bedsteads and mattresses with so many stains on them that at first I think the roof must be leaking. I am not fast enough to grab one of the berths by the door and so end up between Bell and Bloodhound Mush. Bell lies on his bed and winces. 'It's got less springs than a crippled kangaroo,' he moans.

'Get off that bed!' screeches Corporal Martin. His tone

suggests that Bell has been caught in the act of trying to mount his own mother. 'Get fell in outside. Come on. Move! !'

'I'll wear my silk pyjamas tonight,' says Bell as he goes through the door. 'And can you get someone to put a few stitches in the piping on my smoking jacket!'

'Shurrup! !'

Forty minutes later I am back in the barrack room, trying to see round a pile of equipment that I eventually dump on my bed. Most of it is coloured khaki and very little of it looks as if it will fit.

'Take your mess tins and get fell in outside,' says Corporal Martin.

'About time,' says my gloomy companion, thankfully. 'My stomach's beginning to grumble.'

'Wait till you've tasted the nosh. It will be bloody weeping,' retorts Martin with a sadistic grin.

When we get down to the Junior Ranks Restaurant, as I noticed Sergeant Lake was careful to call it, I am reminded of the scene at Melody Bay Holiday Camp where I once used to be a Holiday Host. The solid chomp of two hundred pairs of jaws, long tables, benches, and self service. The only difference is that there are women behind the counter. 'Blimey. Look, birds.'

'You call them birds?'

'More like bleeding vultures.'

'They're W.R.A.C.s.'

'You mean wrecks, don't you?'

Certainly the bints don't have a lot in common with Pan's People but then I never went a lot on judies with turbans and hob nailed boots.

'Let's see how this lot respond to your irresistible magnetism.' Bell is talking to me and there are grunts of agreement from around him.

'I don't want to hog all the talent,' I say modestly.

'Just give us a chance to see how you do it. He'd be doing us a favour, wouldn't he lads?'

'Don't be daft.'

'Come on. You're not shy, are you?'

What can I do? Squaring my enormous shoulders I grasp my mess tins firmly and approach the line of W.R.A.C.s. The first one has got a slash of scarlet for a mouth, or maybe she cut herself shaving. Her finger nails are blacker than a Nigerian's nunga and her complexion so greasy that the blackheads are beginning to slide down to the lower part of her face. Either that or they are being chased there by the invading dandruff.

'Grab a load of Mia Farrow,' says Bell at my elbow. 'She won't know what hit her.'

'Looks as if something has hit her already,' says another joker. 'A truck, most likely.'

'I wonder how much she charges to haunt a house.'

Trying to shut out the audience participation I switch on the famous Lea slow burn and flare my nostrils wider than a poufdah's trouser bottoms.

'Hand over your tin, twat-features,' says the maiden behind the counter. 'I haven't got all fucking night.' She removes something from one of her nostrils and tries to flick it over her shoulder.

'There's posh for you,' breathes Bell.

'Shut your gob.'

'Charming.'

'Piss off!'

'She must be the exception that proves the tool,' says Bell as we help ourselves to a doorstep of bread and a pat of butter that would be pushed to earn a bit part in 'Last Tango in Golders Green'. 'I haven't seen an uglier load of birds since my mother's wedding. They're what I joined the Army to forget.'

'Why did you join the Army?'

'I don't know. It was like getting married, I suppose. It seemed a good idea at the time.'

'Are you married, then?'

'No. I've got no excuse, have I? Are you?'

'Married? Blimey, no.'

'It's a mug's caper, isn't it? Especially these days. Women have got no respect for it, have they? And if they can't be bothered who the heck can? No bloke wants to get lumbered, does he?'

It does not take me long to realise that Bell is a bloke very much after my own heart who talks a lot of sense. In my present situation such allies are hard to find.

The sad-faced fella is called Broom but we call him 'Loogy' after Corporal Martin calls him 'Lugubrious'. We learn that Corporal Martin has been up before an officers' selection board, presumably because he uses words like 'Lugubrious'.

One of the good things about my mum's cooking is that it is so bad that anything else tastes absolutely knock-out. If it had not been for the greasy slag serving it I would be quite enjoying my corned beef fried in deep batter and the semolina, even though they were served in the same tin. These W.R.A.C. birds don't hang about, I can tell you.

The others are more choosy, nor do they take kindly to the washing-up arrangements. A dustbin that looks like an exhibition of vomit through the ages and two tepid vats floating with gunge.

'How is this supposed to work?' asks Loogy.

'You wash it in the first one and sterilise it with a thick layer of grease in the second,' says Bell.

'Up your arse,' says Noel Coward who we discover is called Sculthorpe. He has enjoyed his meal and is currently noshing another slice of bread.

'I wonder why they want us back in the barrack room,' says Loog.

'I expect Sergeant Lake wants to show us how to fold our

pyjamas,' says Bell. In fact, he is not far from being right. The only problem is that when we get back there are very few pairs of pyjamas left. Half our kit has disappeared.

'You should have put it in your lockers,' says Corporal Martin happily. 'That's what they're there for. If you leave anything about in this place it walks.'

'You didn't tell us that when we got the stuff.'

'Don't argue with me! I'm not your bleeding nurse-maid.'

'What are we going to do?'

'You'll have to buy some more.'

'But I don't have any money.'

'It'll be deducted from your pay. Now, belt up and listen to me. I'm going to show you how to fold your bedding and I'm only going to do it once.'

Corporal Martin is even better than his word. He shows us how to fold all our kit. This has to be displayed in our lockers like blooming collectors' items. The whole thing is so diabolically stupid that I keep hoping I am going to wake up and find that I have dozed off on top of Brenda Maidstone – or 'made regularly' as we used to call her back in those good old Scraggs Lane days.

'Right. Now, are there any questions?' says Martin eventually.

'I was thinking—'

'No boasting, Broom. Right, if there's no questions, Sergeant Lake will have a few words with you.'

'Stand up! Sit down! Standup! Sidown!! ASYOUWERE!!! I said "as you were!"'

'I'm going to swing for this bloke,' mutters Bell.

'When I come into the room, everyone stands up. Do you understand me? Do I make myself plain?'

'You don't have to bother, mate,' murmurs Bell. 'You're already the plainest bloke I've ever seen.'

'Is there something you want to say, Bell?'

'No, Sergeant.'

'Well, belt up!'

'Yes, Sergeant.'

'Right. Sit down smartly and listen to me. This is very important. Is there anyone here who has any "O" Levels?'

My hand goes in the air before you can say 'Open University'. O.K. So art and woodwork do not make me Clapham's answer to Albert Einstein, but did he have my physique?

'Right, Lea.' Sergeant Lake looks happy for the first time that I can remember. 'I might have guessed that you would be one of our bright boys.' The rest of the barrack room look at me with a mixture of envy and dislike. I wonder what position of responsibility has been singled out for me? Maybe Mum was right to make me stay on for that extra year. 'I've got just the job for you. You can stamp every man's number on his equipment. The rest of you can get on cleaning your kit.'

'But what about my kit, Sergeant?' I bleat.

'It won't take you so long, with your education. You'll soon catch up once you've finished with the stamps and the stencils.'

'But, Sergeant!'

'No "buts". Get on with it. Corporal Martin will issue you with the necessary utensils.'

'It's a wonderful thing, education,' says Bell, two hours later by which time I have hammered my fingers flatter than one of grandma's tits.

'Piss off.'

'They're blooming insane, these buggers, aren't they? Fancy issuing you with boots with little bumps all over them and then making you smooth them down with a heated spoon handle. You wouldn't credit it, would you?'

It is a fact that all round the room men are sitting in the glow of candles and heating up their spoon handles like it is a Young Conservatives fondu party – or fondle party as they have a habit of becoming.

'I haven't got half-way through these bastards yet,' I bleat.

'Don't worry. Once you've done that you've only got to clean your brasses, polish your boots, blanco your belt and gaiters, press your uniform and the rest of the night is yours, right up to breakfast time.'

'"Right up" all right. By the cringe, I think I'll knot myself!'

'Don't get worked up about it. I'll give you a hand. What's this bloke's number?'

'Two-three-one-two-nine-six-seven-three.'

'Right.' Bell picks up a metal stamp and the hammer, and grabbing hold of a mess tin sprays a row of twos along it. 'There, that cuts it down a bit, doesn't it?'

'But that's not his number.'

'It is now. He'll recognise it and nobody else will have it. Come on, give us the next one.'

In no time we whip through all the numbers from one to nine and find that we only have two more sets of equipment to do. For these we use six, turning it upside down for the last numeral, and then repeating the process making it a nine to start with. Fascinating, isn't it? Oh well, maybe you're right.

About half past eight Sergeant Lake looks in to make sure that we are all suffering and seems surprised that I am now putting the finishing touches to my boots.

'Finished all that equipment, have you, Lea?'

'Yes, Sergeant.'

Fortunately, Misery Guts picks up one of the first items I stamped and can therefore find no fault with it.

'Right,' he says. 'Who wants to go down to the N.A.A.F.— I mean, The Junior Ranks Social Centre?'

Without pausing to think, the stupid fools hurl their mits into the air like he is offering free dips in a bucketful of tight fannies. Only Lea keeps his sticky little pandy at lap level. You can't catch a Lea twice. Never volunteer for anything. I should have remembered that the first time.

'Right, off you go and be back here by twenty-one thirty hours. Where do you think you're going, Lea?'

'I've changed my mind, Sergeant.'

'You should be so lucky! You don't change your underpants without I say so. I have a job for you. There's a little party at the sergeants' mess tonight.'

'Wee Georgie Wood?'

'Right, Bell. You can bring your sense of humour along as well. I need a couple of waiters.'

'The only waiting I've done has been outside the Labour Exchange, Sarge.'

'Sergeant! That doesn't matter. You'll be told what to do.'

'I haven't finished my kit yet.'

'Leave it. You can do it when you come back.'

'Marvellous, isn't it?' says Bell as we stride along behind Watchit. 'Our first night and we're going to a party already. Even the blooming booklet didn't promise you that.'

'I'm knackered,' I say. 'I want to go to sleep.' I mean it, too. Amanda and the journey have taken a lot out of me, without all the bull we have been subjected to.

'It's all right for you. Some of us need a stab at the fur doughnut.'

'You don't really reckon there's going to be any spare about, do you? You must be round the twist.'

'You never know your luck.'

To my surprise there are in fact a fair number of birds standing around the sergeants' mess, and when I say 'fair' I mean ugly. The sergeants are entertaining their opposite numbers in the W.R.A.C.s and they don't win a lot of beauty contests, I can tell you.

'Look at that one,' says Bell. 'Dracula stood her up at the church door.'

'Looks as if he bashed her over the nut with it.'

The female in question – and I mean it is questionable whether she is a female – makes Sonny Liston look like Liza

Minelli. She has shoulders like an all-in wrestler – 'all-in', meaning knackered – and a pair of knockers like the buffers on platform nine at King's Cross. Her complexion reminds me of perished rubber and the arrangement of her features must have been decided by a committee who had five minutes to kill before collecting their expenses. Sergeant Lake is no oil painting and he is wincing as he lets his mince pies sprint across her phizog.

Bell and I have been issued with mess jackets and we belt backwards and forwards between a serving hatch passing on orders. These geezers pour it down like they are putting out a fire in their socks and I work up a thirst watching them. It soon dawns on me that there is no need to go thirsty and I order an extra drink every time I go to the hatch. In this way I am soon as plastered as any piss artist in the room. I notice that 'Tinker' Bell is not far behind me.

'It's not bad, is it? Better than cleaning your bleeding kit.'

'You want to watch it,' I say. 'You're nearly as pissed as I am.'

'I can hold my liquor, mate. Don't you worry about me.' To demonstrate the point Bell slops half a trayful of Scotch onto the carpet.

'Have you seen anything you fancy?' I ask.

'Nothing I'd want to talk to while I was doing it. I don't fancy women in uniform. It's not right. I reckon their tits are tattooed "mild" and "bitter".'

' "Tattooed." I reckon you'd need a pneumatic drill with that lot.'

'Waiter. Get me a Horse's Neck.'

'I think he's trying for the set,' says Bell, indicating the bird the sergeant is talking to. 'She's got a horse collar, I can guarantee it. I reckon you could get stuck in to her and you wouldn't know you were there if it wasn't for the echo.'

'Belt up, you two and get on with your job,' snarls an

unfriendly voice in our ear-holes and we start chasing backwards and forwards again.

As the evening proceeds it becomes obvious that the booze is having the effect it has had since times immoral. Inhibitions, already knee high to an arse hopper, are strewn around the floor like french letters at a church social and an atmosphere of what one might laughingly call romance prevails.

'I reckon this could get interesting,' murmurs Bell reading my mind.

Unfortunately, we are not offered the chance to stick around and find out how interesting.

'Right, you two. You can fall out now,' says Sergeant Lake, dragging his eyes away from a bird who looks as if the hard stuff is beginning to melt her make-up.

'We don't mind staying a bit longer, Sarge.'

'Sergeant! How many times do I have to tell you? This isn't "Dad's Army". You get back and make sure your kit is up to scratch. We can look after ourselves.' He looks at the bird when he says that and you have to have a strong stomach to remain unaffected by the look of sheer naked lust that invades his mug.

'Did you see the corset that bird was wearing?' says Bell as we steal away – we steal away half a bottle of scotch, actually. 'From behind she looked like a skeleton shoved into a rubber stocking.'

'Let's have a little shufti through one of the windows,' I say taking another swig of scotch. 'I want to see what they're getting down to.'

So we nip round the back of the building only to find that all the curtains have been drawn tighter than a gnat's arsehole.

'Bloody spoilsports,' says Bell.

'Look, there's a crack, up there.'

'Blimey, are they swinging from the chandeliers already?'

'No, you berk. I mean a gap in the curtains, don't I? Right

at the top. You stand on the window ledge and I'll support you.'

Bell pulls himself up on the ledge and I hold his legs and wait for reports.

'What are they doing?'

'Wait a minute, I can't – oh, yes. They've taken the sheet off the billiards table. Blimey!'

'What is it? What are they doing?!' I croak.

But I never get the chance to find out. A torch starts flashing behind us and an upper class voice starts trilling in our ear-holes.

'Hey! You two! What the deuce do you think you're doing? Come here!'

'Run for it!' Bell does not have a lot of alternative because I do not wait for a reply but start legging it towards the nearest line of huts. I hear him hit the ground as I belt round the corner of a pile of coke.

'Come back!!' screeches a voice sounding both angry and surprised. Bell rushes round the corner and nearly jumps out of his skin when I grab his arm.

'Thanks for waiting! You're a blooming fine mate, aren't you? I might have broken my bloody leg.'

'I was just doing a little recce. Come on, this way.' We run down a row of darkened billets, and then – blimey! There is another torch flashing in front of us.

'We'll have to hide.' Our eyes bounce off the surrounding landscape and I notice a barrack room door that is slightly open. 'In here.' We dart inside and there are two rows of sleeping bodies. Outside can be heard the sound of running footsteps. 'Under the beds.' My hooter collides with the floor and I wriggle under the nearest fluff trap. Above me a body stirs and I turn my head sideways to avoid the sagging springs. It is funny but I can see a brassière hanging from the knob of the bedside locker. A trophy, I suppose.

An arc of light spreading across the floor tells me that the door has opened. 'Excuse me, ladies. You haven't seen a couple of men in here, have you?'

Before I can totally grasp the significance of that remark a female voice speaks from above me. 'No such bleeding luck, mate. Have you got a couple to spare?'

'They were seen hanging around the sergeants' mess.'

'Why don't you hang around here yourself? And bring your mate in with you.'

'We'll soon stop you hanging,' says another female voice.

Could it be? Is it possible that—? No, it can't be. Yet, perhaps. Who knows? Maybe— (Get on with it! Ed. Sorry, T.L.) We must have blundered into the W.R.A.C. sleeping quarters – they are called that because they don't do anything by halves. (Get it? Halves? Quarters? Oh, forget it!)

'We've got a job to do,' says a worried male voice.

'You can get on the job with me any time you like,' says a female voice from the next-door bed.

There is no doubt about it. We are trapped in the midst of the man-eating W.R.A.C.s. For a second I flirt with the idea of giving myself up and then I think of Sergeant Lake and change my mind. When he smiles it looks like a bag full of arseholes exploding and I don't want to get on the wrong side of him – not that any of his sides looks particularly good.

'If you see anyone, let us know.'

'You'll be lucky.' It is the bird above me who is talking and as she rabbits, her mit dangles over the side of the bed and collides with my dicky dirt. Almost in the same movement she starts feeling the contours of my body and her fingers dart down to Percy's parlour. This is it, I think. Any second now she will scream the place down and it will be 'Goodbye Timothy' for another couple of years. I hold my breath but soon that is not the only thing that is being held. 'If I find anything, I'm hanging on to it,' says the saucy cow and, so help me, she flips open my fly and grabs a handful of willing flesh. It is all I can do to keep my mouth shut.

'Don't joke about it,' says the sour male voice. 'I'm serious.'

'So am I.' Percy gets a gentle tweak and responds like a starving moggy being thrown into a vat of cream. He is practically having it away with one of the bed springs and it occurs to me that anyone looking under the bed could jump to a few very unfortunate conclusions.

'We'll be off then.' The voice sounds relieved. 'You know where to find us if you need us.'

'You're never where I want you when I need you.'

'Goodnight.'

'Goodnight, sexy.'

The door closes and there are a few moments of silence during which the pressure on my action man kit does not lessen.

'What are you doing, Brenda?' says a voice from the next bed. 'Brenda!!'

'Look what I've found,' says my new friend who must have spent her formative years on a test-your-grip machine.

The time has obviously come for me to say thank you and goodnight. Not without difficulty I liberate Percy and wriggle out from under the bed.

'Thanks a lot, girls,' I whisper. 'We'll do the same for you one day.'

'You're not going.' I would like to be able to insert a question mark at the end of those four words but it is not possible.

'I've got to get back and finish my kit,' I whine. 'We've only just got here.'

'I can see that by your hair.' The bird runs her steely fingers through my barnet and takes a deep breath. She is not bad looking really and is wearing a shortie night dress which is like one of those frilly things you put round Christmas cakes. I can see that it is short because she has thrown back the bedclothes, giving me a quick flash of her muff in the process.

'Yes, well–er, we'd better be getting along,' I whimper, managing to get my shirt zipped up in my trousers.

'What's the hurry?' Another bird drapes herself across the door.

'Like I said, we've got to—'

'Watch out the M.P.s don't get you. That's right. You heard what the man said: "If you see anyone, let us know." '

'Yeah, but you wouldn't—'

'We might, mightn't we girls?' There are a lot of heads nodding round the barrack room.

'It could be very nasty, couldn't it? Attempted rape on your first night in the army.'

'Attempted rape? We haven't touched anyone.'

Brenda shakes her head. 'No, you haven't, have you?' She stretches back on the bed and draws up her legs. 'Nobody would believe you, though, would they?' The bird in the bed opposite suddenly seizes the front of her nightdress and rips it down to the navel. 'You swine!' she hisses at Bell.

Bell starts back in surprise, topples over the next bed and – it is almost too horrible to relate. What happens next is like dropping a goldfish into a tank full of pirhana. Before you can say 'Grievous bodily harm' half a dozen birds have leapt on to him and his nut chokers are resting on top of a pile of the rest of his clothing. The speed at which they can move is terrifying. His mouth opens to cry out but Brenda is swift to offer a few words of advice. 'Remember the Military Police,' she says. 'I reckon you'd get ten years for what you're about to do.'

'About to do?' croaks Bell.

'You know what Confucius says? "Lie back and enjoy it. You've got an opportunity most men only dream about." '

'That's right, dearie,' says another eager lady shedding her night attire to reveal that she obviously poses for Michelin tyre advertisements. 'Let's all have a nice time.'

'That's right, Tinker. Don't be a spoilsport,' I say loyally. 'You know you've been waiting for a chance like this.'

'And you,' says Brenda.

'I beg your pardon,' I say, reading the look in her eyes.

'Get 'em off. You can start rolling on this side of the room. And don't over-tax yourself to begin with. There are nine girls looking for satisfaction.'

'Eight,' says a disappointed voice from the end of the room.

'Eight!?' I squeal. 'You must be joking. Let's not be ridiculous about this. We've all had a good laugh, now let me leave you with my friend Private Bell. I'm certain that—'

'Take your trousers off or I'll scream the place down and say you raped me.'

'Which end would you like me to start?'

I mean! What can I do? With a record that is worse than Jimmy Osmond singing 'Long Haired Lover from Liverpool' what chance have I got of avoiding another long stretch in the nick? Better a short stretch with the military misses.

'You can start with me, Cuddles.'

'Cuddles', huh. No woman has ever called me that before. I drop my trousers and search Brenda's face for a hint of mercy. Not a chance. I might as well expect to find the hammer and sickle tattooed on Ted Heath's chest.

'You can come under the bedclothes if you're shy.'

There is a hiss of disapproval but I gratefully bundle under the blankets and find Brenda's hungry mouth leeching on to my own. She kisses like she is trying to suck the wrapper off a bullseye and her crutch level radar soon locates unsuspecting Percy. 'Search and destroy' might be the message it sends out. Before you can say 'Roger Carpenter' I have disappeared into her like a collar stud down a plug hole and her pelvis is rotating like she is standing in for a local flour mill. I hang on for grim death and try and think about Harold Wilson's alpenstock, or anything, to stop me from boiling over. If I have seven more like her to get through I need to restrain myself.

Fortunately Brenda goes off faster than a tin of snoek in a heat wave and the second I hear the death rattle beginning to build up at the back of her throat my feet are hitting the floor. Given half a chance they would be guiding me to the door, but Brenda's next door neighbour is swift to pounce. 'Wanda,' she breathes by way of introduction and loses no time in letting her hands show me how she got her name. Having checked that my equipment is still in working order she pulls me down on top of her and sinks her fangs into my shoulder.

'I want to put my mark on you,' she hisses passionately.

I never go a bundle on scratchers and biters and tonight I cannot afford to be roughed up too much.

'Watch it,' I say. 'Don't get carried away in case I do.'

'Despoil me,' she hisses. 'Treat me like the lowest whore in Christendom.' She has obviously been reading too many James Bond books. You can tell that a mile off.

'Don't be a nana,' I tell her. 'I'm not here for my holidays, you know.' I can see she is going to go on a bit so I send her down two of my right hand men to do a recce and plunge into her furry loofah like a clammy khasi pilot on piece work.

'Oh, no,' she says. 'No, no, no, no, NO!' All the time she is saying that she is pulling me on to her like someone trying to force one and a half pounds of rump steak up a drain pipe. I don't know what she does when she is telling you to piss off. I am soon in trouble because the minute a bird hits a big attack of the moanies, Percy starts getting all sentimental and I can sense that a slight weight loss in the Y-front area is a good deal nearer than Christmas. I try to think about athletes foot in a nudists' camp but it is no good. This bird could clear a blocked-up drain by looking at it and when my feet hit the floor Percy is nestling against my goolies like he is trying to hatch them.

'Are you all right, dear?' says a kindly voice from bed number three.

'He's lovely,' says Wanda with feeling. I stop her feeling and stagger towards my next appointment with stress failure. How long can I keep this up?

The same thought is obviously occurring to the lady at the end of the row.

'Leave something for me,' she sings out. 'Don't exhaust him.'

'He'll be safe with me,' says the inmate of bed number three. 'Cuddle up close, ducky love. We'll soon have you in the straight and narrow.' I don't know where she gets the 'narrow' from. When I eventually introduce my spam ram to her spasm chasm it is like sending a rocket ship on a trip into outer space – or inner space, more like.

Fortunately, bed number four throws up a chick called Norma who is so eager to grab a slice of the action that she vaults aboard the flesh fest and lends her not inconsiderable talents to the task of giving Percy a sense of responsibility. Like they say at the Chinese electrician's: many hands make light work. Norma's subtle fingers were obviously intended for better things than scraping mashed potatoes off a spatula in the Junior Ranks Restaurant and soon I am more confused than a worm in a can of spaghetti. Talk about being bombarded with sensations, the Sunday papers would be pushed to do better. By the time I have finished with those two birds I don't know if I've been nibbled or nobbled. Both, I reckon.

Four down and four to go. Blimey, I would have bought a bar of chocolate if I had known.

I take a butchers across the room and see that Bell is still trapped on bed number two. Either he is giving better value for money than me or is meeting stiffer resistance. By the time I am dragged onto bed number five my piece of resistance is certainly not stiff.

'Can I come back next week?' I gulp.

'Unless you get on with it you won't be able to come back

next week,' snarls a voice which is obviously in no mood for disappointment. 'One scream from me and the only time you'll be leaving the guard room is for your court-martial.'

'Give me a few minutes, then. I'm not a bloody machine.' It always gets right up my bracket that birds should be able to go on for ever like battery operated fire-crackers while us blokes have to lie around listening to them moaning for action. It makes me think of all the times I have had a hard on and never the chance to use it. Like when you don't want a copper, the bastards are falling out of the trees. Now that I need some penis power my old man is like a ripple on a saucer of cream.

'No need to waste your time while you're waiting,' says the saucy minx. 'I had a bath tonight.' If I had any difficulty working out what she was getting at she makes it easy for me by pushing down the bed clothes, pulling up her nightie and showing me what is on the menu. I have nothing against a spot of muff diving but I am not sure I want to indulge before a barrack room full of birds. It is putting a bit of a strain on my natural sense of delicacy. 'Right, if that's the best you can do then I might as well give my lungs a bit of exercise.'

That does it. I am administering the kiss of life before you can say 'don't talk with your mouth full'.

Fortunately, Percy finds it almost as stimulating to give as to receive and I am able to finish off number five with a spot of pelvis pumping and still retain my deposit. I never find out what the bird's name is but it doesn't worry me overmuch as I don't intend to send her a bunch of flowers in the morning. I don't ask much from a woman, but a little common civility helps – even downright vulgar civility is better than nothing.

I hit number six before Percy has time to get cheesed off and I must confess that she is quite a nice little article. Dresden china compared to some of them. She grabs hold of you like a bad habit and from the feel of her it is quite possible to believe that she has not indulged in a gang bang with the Congolese Cavalry. Like a tightly coiled velvet spring, it is, rather than the inside of an elephant's trunk. She is also a very excitable little creature and, as I have said before, a spot of audience participation is always a help, isn't it? One is grateful to see that one's efforts are being appreciated. This bird shivers like a hundred and ten pounds of jelly in a tornado and the noise she makes is even louder than the sound of Bell screaming for mercy across the other side of the room. It is just as well that poor Tinker is up against it – or not up against it, as is more nearly the case – because the sound of him rabbiting on diverts my attention from the owner of the punctured minge fringe currently wriggling on the end of my sunshine stick. I am not president of the local sperm bank and cannot afford to be taken out of myself at this stage of the game. Game! I would laugh hollowly if I had the strength.

'Hurry up, I can't wait much longer!' pants the bint in the next bed.

'Carry on without me,' I croak. 'I'll try and catch up with you, later.'

This course of action is clearly not to the lady's liking but fortunately a back-throat yodel from my current sparring partner tells me that my responsibilities are discharged – and darn nearly not the only thing, either.

As I cross the floor I feel like a marathon runner entering the stadium and the image is sustained when I hit the lower tum of the judy in bed number seven. Talk about an echo chamber. Compared to her an aircraft hangar would be like the inside of a shoe box.

'OOOh! That feels smashing,' she gloats. I am glad she can feel something. I reckon I would be pushed to touch the sides if I folded my old man in half. After all I have been through it is not surprising really, I suppose.

In order to keep my pecker up I chuck in a few groans of my own and Percy is so stupid that he imagines he is having a marvellous time and responds like a daft dog fishing sticks out of a pond.

I count up to twenty in roman numerals and the lady with a heart as big as all outdoors and a twat to match, goes into orbit. Another satisfied customer! At this rate they might hang on to me for the regimental mascot. Bell, they could drape over one of the drums. He is in bed number four on the other side of the room and he does not look as if he is going to get out of it. I have seen more action watching a mosquito sprint across a slice of treacle pudding.

'Are you all right, mate?' I hiss.

'What did he do in civvy street?' says one of the birds scornfully. 'Work in a steam laundry? He's all washed out.'

'You'd better get over here sharpish,' says another bird. The words strike cold terror into my heart – and more southerly regions – because the bint is talking to me! Is it possible that female nature could plumb such depths? Of course it is. You don't have to take out a year's subscription to 'True Romances' to know the answer to that one. Your grade one oggins-hungry bird is not easily robbed of her prey.

To my surprise relief arrives from an unexpected quarter. Brenda is swift to speak her mind.

'He belongs to us,' she says. 'You've got your own bloke. It's not our fault he's duff. Before ours does anything he's going to give us seconds first.'

That is it! The minute I hear those words I wish I had a cut throat razor in my hand. I would put myself beyond the reach of the perishing lot of them.

'That's typical!' snaps a voice from the bed next to Bell. 'We never get a fair crack at the wick.'

'Rubbish! You don't know anything about the arts of love, that's your trouble. You don't know how to coax the best out of a man.'

I feel like joining in the belly laugh that greets that one but I am too exhausted. Also, it is difficult to laugh when your face is buried in the middle of a mobile knocker factory.

The bird in bed number eight is sobbing because she is temporarily out of action – either that or she can't bear to see what they are doing to me – and the inmate of number nine moves with remarkable speed for a large woman. And when I say large I don't mean Mama Cass I mean 'Excuse me, but can you direct me to the other half of the elephant act?' She snatches me into her hungry arms and scuttles back to her bed like a two-ton spider. I am beyond resistance and can only lie gasping for breath as she massages me into her body like a jar of Sloan's linament. When you have a bird with as many ruckles of flesh as she has got it is difficult to know quite what is happening. In my case it is very little, but the lady seems grateful to have anything at all. When I take a quick butchers at her mug I can see why. Blimey! What a disgusting sight. I am better off being suffocated between her bristols. I dive back into her flesh bunker and let her get on with it.

I don't know what she normally gets up to in that bed but it rattles like a tray of tin tacks. That coupled with Big Bertha's happy shudders and a few piebald comments from the rest of the barrack room make it seem like New Year's Eve in The Dug and Dick. If the M.P.s are still about they will be through the door like a dose of salts. There is no point in me subjecting myself to the threat of instant heart failure any longer. I can get out with impunity – and anyone else who wants to come. Big B. lets out a disgusting gurgle like dirty bath water disappearing down the plug hole and I know that my debt to society has been paid.

'O.K.,' I say menacingly, vaulting from the bed. 'I'm getting out of here and I wouldn't try and stop me if I were you.'

There is an ugly rumble from a number of ugly throats and a groan from Bell. 'Get off him,' I tell the buxom charmer engaged in hammering his dongler up to his rib cage. 'He's coming with me.'

'You go on,' groans my comrade. 'I don't think I'll be able to make it.'

'You can say that again,' scoffs his attacker. 'I don't think he's ever made it.'

'Get away from that door,' I tell Brenda. 'We're going through and nothing is going to stop us.'

'I'll scream.'

'Scream the place down. Right now I really fancy a nice, quiet cell.' I may be mistaken but I think Bell is sobbing. The poor devil! What have they done to him?

'Are you ready, girls?' Brenda opens her large trap and there is a sharp intake of breath around me.

'Come on, Tinker.' I help my stricken comrade to his feet and guide his unsteady footsteps towards the door. What a shame I haven't the strength left to whistle the march from 'The Bridge Over the River Kwai'.

'H-e-e-ell-l—' I would like to be able to report that Brenda belts up because I catch her a fourpenny one across the cake-hole but this is regrettably not the case. Just as I am approaching her not ungenerous curves the hut door flies open and two blokes are revealed standing shoulder to shoulder in the doorway.

I am about to throw myself down on my knees to give thanks when I see that it is not two blokes. It is the enormous W.R.A.C. Sergeant who was at the sergeants' mess party. 'Ho, ho. What have we here?' she says. 'Been interfering with my little chickadees, have you?'

'No, no,' I shriek. 'My friend felt faint as we were passing and we came in for a glass of water.'

A gasp of amazed outrage goes up at this remark.

'Blooming lies!' hisses Brenda. 'You only have to look at them to see why they came here.'

'I was going to ask if it was necessary to take off all your clothes to drink a glass of water,' says the Sergeant.

'We're very messy drinkers,' I explain.

'It was horrible,' snivels treacherous Wanda. 'They-they-attacked us.'

'Only in self defence,' croaks Bell. 'They said they'd scream for the M.P.s unless we went to bed with them.'

'I don't know how you have the gall to say that.'

'Because it's the bleeding truth, that's why!'

'Silence, all of you.' Sergeant Big waves an arm at Bell and myself. 'You two come with me. The rest of you try to shut out this harrowing experience and get some sleep. Have no fear, the malefactors will be punished.'

'What's a malefactor, Sergeant?' asks one of the bints.

'An evil doer.'

'That's him all right,' says the bird indicating Bell. 'He was—' She suddenly realises what she is saying and belts up.

'Try not to think about it,' says the Sergeant sympathetically. She jerks her finger at us. 'Get your clothes on and get outside, you scum. You're going to get what's coming to you.'

'Oh, my gawd!' moans Bell.

We struggle into our threads and out of the billet. I crack my ankle against one of the beds and I am hobbling worse than Bell by the time we begin to stumble down the row of huts.

'Did you attack those girls?' accuses Sergeant Big.

'No!' squeals Bell. 'They must have very vivid imaginations or something.'

'Are you sure?' The Sergeant has stopped outside a hut set back from the others. She opens the door with a key and shoos us inside. It occurs to me that she is fairly well pissed. I wonder why she is not bothering to put on the light.

'We never laid a finger on them,' I say. 'We wouldn't, would we? It would be stupid to try and have it away with a whole room full of birds.'

'Insane,' chokes Bell. I think he has started crying again.

'You could get three years for just being in that billet,' says our large captor, menacingly. By the cringe, but she is ugly. Especially when she starts unbuttoning her tunic – hey! Wait a minute. What does she think she is doing?

'I should hand you over,' she says. 'But I can understand how, faced by that bevy of beauty, your natural appetites got the better of you. You must be very frustrated.'

'Frustrated!' croaks Bell.

'You didn't touch them, did you?' says Sergeant Big suspiciously.

'No! Of course not,' shrieks Bell. I don't say anything because I am too busy looking at the hairy armpits revealed when she takes her blouse off.

'Right. You lucky boys can appease your lust on me.'

'Yerwhat?' says Bell.

'I'm prepared to turn a blind eye this time.' Now come to think about it she does look as if she has got a glass eye. 'Don't just stand there, otherwise I'll think you don't fancy me.'

'Well—'

'—And then it would have to be down to the guardroom.'

'Oh, blimey,' says Bell. 'What are we going to do?'

'I don't know,' I say, starting to remove my trousers. 'I expect we'll think of something.'

CHAPTER FOUR

When reveille sounds my eyes are stuck together tighter than an Irish nun's thighs at a wake. I cannot think of another moment in my life when I have felt so knackered. The sound of that bleeding bugle seems to be fed to me intravenously.

At least I am back in my own barrack room again. When I think of what went on in Sergeant Toogood's room – yeah, that was the bird's name. Fantastic, isn't it? – a hot flush sprints through my system a couple of times. Call me bashful, if you like – call me Celia BigJobs if it really turns you on – but there are some things that even I draw the line at describing. Tinker Bell and I will carry the secret of the hut of shame with us to the grave.

'Hands off cocks, hands on socks.' Witty Corporal Martin is present to help anyone who has trouble doing up his buttons.

I stagger out to the washroom and take a discreet butchers at my action man kit. It practically whimpers as I touch it and looks like it has been worried by a pack of fox hounds. What a diabolical way to go. I can honestly say that I never want to see another piece of totty again. I am right back to where I was in chapter one. Physically wrecked. 'Your kit is a bleeding disgrace, Lea.'

'Is that bleeding, too?' Corporal Martin does not understand my little joke but there is no doubt that he has a point – which is more than I have. My boots have still got more pimples than the before part of an acne advertisement and the only creases on my uniform are those made when I fell asleep in it.

'You'd better skip breakfast and do something about it, otherwise Sergeant Lake will have your guts for garters.'

I accept that the two-striped twit has a point and settle down with Bell while the rest of the barrack room are marched down to the cookhouse – everyone has given up trying to call it the Junior Ranks Restaurant.

'I don't think I'll ever—'

'No. Neither will I. And don't blanco your beret, it doesn't do anything for it.' Poor Bell is out on his feet. He can hardly keep his eyes open and is moving his mit backwards and forwards like he is stroking a pet rabbit.

'Sod it! I didn't realise what I was doing.'

'Give it here. You'll never finish it, carrying on like that.' I grab hold of his belt and, blow me, if two minutes later he isn't stretched out on his bed gonking like a good 'un. I suppose Toogood did indicate her preference for him in a rather demonstrative fashion but there is no excuse for an Egyptian P.T. display at this hour of the morning.

'Stop cuddling your cock and get on with your bed roll,' I tell him. 'They're going to be back from breakfast in a minute.'

'What!?' Bell sits up with a start and darts a terrified glance round the room as if expecting to see someone. Certainly his experience with Sergeant Toogood was very harrowing – not to mention ploughing, sowing, reaping and threshing.

'Hello, lads. I bought you a jam butty.' Loogy returns with the rest of the intake and hands over a couple of folded slices of bread and jam.

'God bless, mate.' I accept the offering and watch a generous dollop of raspberry jam drop onto my bedding. Loogy gets all worked up about it but I tell him not to get his knickers in a twist. It seems the least of my worries at the time. Sergeant Lake takes the matter more seriously.

'You reaching puberty, are you Lea?' he snarls. 'Or was it an unsuccessful suicide attempt?'

'Neither, Sergeant.'

'If you want to kill yourself you have to get permission, you know.'

'Yes, Sergeant.'

'In your case you shouldn't have any difficulty.'

'No, Sergeant.'

'Your only problem will be to get the blood to run out of your body. I doubt if it could crawl out on its hands and knees without breaking into a sweat! You're idle, Lea!'

'Yes, Sergeant.'

'Your kit is a bleeding disgrace. I've seen fuzzy wuzzies better turned out than you.'

'I didn't have time, Sergeant.'

'"Didn't have time!" You were specially selected for recreational training at the sergeants' mess in order to restore you for the task in hand and you have betrayed my trust. I feel very bad about it, Lea.'

I don't feel so good myself but I keep quiet about it.

'The whole barrack room is a disgrace, but you – and you! Wake up, lad!' Bell has his eyes closed and is beginning to rock backwards and forwards.

'—Are in a class by yourselves. I've never seen anything like it. Never, anything like it, have I seen!' The pitch at which he delivers the last word makes Maria Callas sound like Paul Robeson. 'It is so horrible I can't bear to look at it.' He sweeps all my hastily folded kit onto the floor and boots it across the room. 'Tomorrow morning this barrack room is going to be inspected by your platoon commander, Lieutenant Bland. And he will crucify me if he finds it in this condition. And if he crucifies me I'm going to disembowel Corporal Martin. And if I disembowel Corporal Martin he's going to cut off your arms and legs and beat you over the head with them.'

'It all sounds terribly messy,' says a refined voice from the other end of the room.

'Shurrup! ! It's not funny.' Sergeant Lake breathes heavily like a boxer taking a break between rounds. 'There's got to be a thousand per cent improvement in this billet. Do you understand?'

'Yes, Sergeant.'

'Right. Today, you're going to get your hair cut. Stop groaning! It's just a little trim to stop you looking like a load of fairies. You'll probably find things you'd given up for lost years ago. Like your ears. After that its drill, regimental history, drill, P.T., drill and drill. Any questions?'

'Yes, Sergeant. How do you report sick?'

'Are you taking the mickey again, Bell?'

'No, Sarge – I mean Sergeant. I—'

'You haven't been in the Army long enough to report sick. I'll tell you when you're ill, Bell. At the moment you're idle that's your trouble. Do you understand me?'

'Yes, Sergeant.'

'Right. Fall in outside, the lot of you. And remember what I said. At the moment you're a disgrace to the Queen's uniform. If she saw you she'd be weeping all over her corgies.'

We are marched round to the barber's and it is obvious that our destination is no secret to the shaven-headed squaddies we pass en route.

'Give us a kiss, sailor.' 'O-o-o-o-h, Duckie!' 'Don't stand on his hair, Sarge!'

'Up your arse,' says Sculthorpe, dependably.

I fancy an Army haircut rather less than probing an electric fan with my dick and my mood is not improved when I see the geezer responsible for wielding the clippers. He is a dead ringer for those blokes you used to find hanging about tree stumps with bloodstained axes in their mits. All he needs is a black mask for you to feel distinctly light-headed. He looks as if it would hurt him to smile and there is more hair round his chair than at a sheep shearing contest.

We huddle on the benches which surround the room and try and avoid his eye. This is not so difficult because his eyes make a good job of avoiding each other.

'You,' he says. and two blokes get up. He is in fact trying

to attract someone else's attention and a bloke with hair breaking over his collar creeps into the chair.

'How do you like it, son?' asks Sweeney Sod, not unkindly.

'Just a trim,' says the poor basket nervously. 'Fairly long at the sides and perhaps a bit off the top.'

'A bit off the top, eh? Right.'

Squeamish readers would do well to skip the next couple of lines. What follows is enough to scare the raisins out of your mince pies. The demon barber grabs a handful of hair, lifts it towards the ceiling and then dives in with his clippers. Like a bleeding combine harvester cutting a swathe through a field of corn, the clippers go right down to the flesh.

'It's like a bleeding poodle parlour,' hisses Loogy. I turn to Bell but he has fallen asleep with his head on Sculthorpe's shoulder.

'I think I'm going to be sick,' says the bloke with the refined voice.

What Sweeney Sod does to that bloke would encourage Yul Brynner to audition for the cast of 'Hair'. I can hardly bear to look at him. When it comes to my turn I feel like knotting myself. I never reckoned myself a lot of competition to Clint Eastwood – but, Blimey! Unless birds start getting hot for coconuts I might as well chuck my action kit in the deep freeze for a couple of years. Not, of course, that I ever want to bring Percy into contact with another minge fringe, oh dear me, no. In my present mood I feel more like making an attack on the world aspirin swallowing record.

'Right!' Sergeant Lake's voice reveals that he is chuffed to bollocks with our current misery. 'Now that you are all several pounds lighter and can hear me when I'm speaking to you, say hello to your ears and get fell in, outside! I'm going to make soldiers of you if it kills me. If it kills you that's a different matter.'

'He's a blooming laugh riot, isn't he?' says Bell. 'I don't know what I'd do without him—'

'—but you'd rather. Yeah, I know. Isn't it wonderful that we share the same sense of humour?'

'Don't take the piss.'

'Were you at Oxford, too?'

'Shurrup, you two!! Sculthorpe, you're going to be right marker.'

'Lucky old Sculthorpe. Teacher's pet, eh?'

'Up your arse!'

'One thing about Sculthorpe: you really know where you are with him, don't you?'

'Up your arse!!'

'Must have been a wrench to leave the diplomatic corps and join up with a lot of coarse buggers like us.'

'Up your—!!!'

'RIGHT MARKER!'

Sergeant Lake drives us up and down the barrack square like he wants us to make a hole in the concrete and I am feeling about as sprightly as a dead skunk's armpit when we are brought to a ragged halt.

'Diabolical! There's no other word for it! You're the worst intake I've ever had. Do you hear me? The worst!' Sergeant Lake rages on. 'Your chances in the inter-platoon competition are lower than a ferret's arsehole.'

'He's a lovely talker, isn't he?' says Bell, who seems to be perking up with the exercise.

'Shut your gob, unless you want to be on another fizzer!'

We continue to belt up and down and I notice that a spindly officer-type gink is watching us from the edge of the square. His hat is tipped low over his eyes and his hands are folded behind his back. Thanks to the fact that he does not have a chin it is obviously possible for him to do up his front collar stud without looking in the mirror. Very handy when you are on manoeuvres, I reckon.

'I see Mark Phillips has turned up,' says Bell out of the corner of his mouth. 'Hardly recognise him without the horse, would you?'

'Plat-o-o-n SHUN!' Lakey brings us to a halt, turns us left after two attempts and twists his mouth into the right position for speech. 'Right. Your platoon commander is about to approach you. Lieutenant Bland. Remember that name. B-L-A-N-D. Bland as in mild or balmy. I mean of course, B-A-L-M-Y not B-A-R-M-Y.'

Something deep down inside suggests to me that Sergeant Lake does not think that Lieutenant Bland is the best thing to hit the Army since The Small Arms Training Manual. We titter dutifully and watch Lieutenant Bland's lean frame sway towards us.

'Stand the men at ease, Sergeant.' Bland returns the salute in a more leisurely fashion and removes a gob of spittle from one of his mince pies.

Lakey does as he is told with the maximum of screeching and quivering and Bland fixes what is presumably meant to be a reassuring smile on his mug.

'Thank you, Sergeant,' he says. He has a voice that makes a radio announcer sound like Arthur English and I reckon he must keep half a pound of plums at the back of his north and south. I have nothing against people who talk posh but I do like to be able to understand what they are saying. 'My name is Bland. Lieutenant Bland. I expect that Sergeant Lake has told you that I am your platoon commander and as such responsible for your moral and physical welfare. If you have any problems bring them to me. That's what I'm here for. Right, Sergeant?' Lakey manages to look as if it is the first time that anyone has told him what Lieutenant Bland is there for. 'I know it's easy in these early days to feel a bit lost. The Army is a big place and you – you are – er,' Sergeant Lake closes his eyes, 'only a small part of it. But remember: small parts can do their bit when the time comes. Work hard and play hard and you'll get a lot out of life at Westery. You've come to a regiment with wonderful traditions and I want you all to be determined to prove yourself worthy of them. "First in, last out." That's the

Loamshire's motto and it doesn't only apply to the cook-house.' Sergeant Lake turns his wince into a sickly smile as he finds Bland looking at him, expectantly. 'We may seem a bit strange at first, eh Sergeant?' Lakey nods slowly. 'But you'll soon get used to us. Remember, we're here to help. I want you to look on me as a father.'

'Gordon Bennet!'

'Watch it!!' Sergeant Lake roams up and down the front rank like an alsatian begging to be slipped its lead.

'Any problems, come and see me. Sergeant Lake will tell you where to go. Rightyho, carry on, Sergeant.'

'SAH!!' Lieutenant Bland collects another face full of gob lather before drifting across the square. I notice that his fly buttons are undone.

'Right. You know what to do if you have any problems. I have problems, too. YOU LOT!!' Sergeant Lake is reaching for the high notes again and does not stop screeching until he falls us out half an hour later.

'What a bastard he is,' grunts Bell. 'What did you think of Barmy Bland?'

'All right. Bit of a pouf. I don't fancy him as my old man.'

'I don't fancy him as anyone's old man. He doesn't look the parts, does he?'

'I never reckon anyone who talks like that can get his end away. But they must be able to, mustn't they? Otherwise there wouldn't be so many of them around.'

'I can never understand why they don't have any chins.'

'It's because of all the inbreeding. If you're a toff you're so fussy about who you get hitched to that you don't like going outside your own family. Also, it helps when you're looking down your nose at people. There's nothing to get in the way.'

The next few days pass slower than a constipated elephant and I have callouses on my callouses from all the bulling I have to do to catch up with the other bastards. It is a strange fact of human nature that although they will grumble like buggery about the bullshit, my fellow trainees are always thinking up new ways of making more for themselves. Some prick decides to paint the knobs on the end of his bed so everybody has to do it. Next thing you know is that Sculthorpe has painted a white line on the floor round his bed. Corporal Martin prefers this to the Mona Lisa, so, once again, we all have to do it.

Sculthorpe is definitely establishing himself as a grade one pain in the arse. His vocabulary does not get any bigger but he is keen as a tart on overtime and could beat a caterpillar at crawling. Fortunately, he is thick as two short planks and this is something that Bell and I can turn to advantage when we do our first exercise outside the camp.

Sergeant Lake brings us the glad tidings.

'Right. I expect you are all eager to get through the camp gates and experience some of the North Shropshire Dolce Vita?' he beams.

'That's some kind of cheese, isn't it?' says Loogy. There is a ripple of enthusiasm from the rest of the barrack room. Poor fools, will they never learn?

'Yes, Sergeant!'

'Well, you're going to get the chance this afternoon. A nice little exercise to test your ability to find your way from A to B and see a bit of the local countryside.' Faces begin to fall faster than lead raindrops. 'You will be taken out and dropped in small groups equal distances from the camp. You will then make your way back to the camp by foot. Two points: by foot and back to the camp. We had a soldier in the last intake with a very confused sense of direction. He ended up in Liverpool. He's back with us now, though. In the guardroom. Let that be a lesson to you. Control your wanderlust. I understand that Lieutenant Bland is offering a small prize for the first team home.'

'He's a very lovely human being,' mutters Bell.

I am not insane about the countryside and have hardly

seen any of it since I worked as a driving instructor at Cromingham, emergent jewel of the north Norfolk coast. Nevertheless anywhere is better than row upon row of semicircular corrugated iron huts and I am soon gazing out of the back of the truck like someone gave me *The Observer's Book of British Birds* for my birthday. We speed down a few narrow lanes with the tall hedges scuffing the sides of the lorry and then pull out into rolling grassland. There are cows and all that kind of thing, and another view of the mountains in the background.

'Bleeding holiday camp, this place,' sniffs Lake. 'You should be paying the Army to come here.'

Nobody answers him, maybe because, like me, they are lapping up a glimpse of a tent parked at the edge of a field. Two birds in bikinis are poncing about outside and there is no doubt that they are a sight for sore eyes – or sore thighs, as is the case with me. Although completely off sex I am not averse to the sight of a few tastefully arranged limbs. What true child of nature would be?

'Right, Lea, Bell and—' Sergeant Lake pauses to allow a malevolent smile to spread across his mug '—Sculthorpe. We're dropping you here. No need for the rest of you to start autographing your underwear. You're all going to have an equal chance. The distances have all been scrupulously worked out by Mr Bland.'

'Where is Lieutenant Bland, Sergeant?'

'Call him Mr Bland, Belchamber. You always address junior officers as if they were civilians. Maybe it's some kind of wish fulfilment.'

'I don't understand, Sergeant.'

'Don't let it worry you, Belchamber. Mr Bland is exercising his horse. It was very nice of him to find the time to come and see us the other day.'

'Do we all have a chance to ride, Sergeant?'

'No, Belchamber. The only thing you get on is my nerves.'

Witty Sergeant Lake bangs on the back of the driver's cab and the truck squeals to a halt.

'Right. Out you get. And remember what I said. Don't get any ideas about sending me a postcard from Monte Carlo. You keep an eye on them, Sculthorpe.'

Sculthorpe's pigeon chest swells with pride. He was the only bloke who needed no more than a trim at the barber's and can obviously see himself with a Field Marshal's baton in his rucksack. I can see him with one somewhere else but I keep my thoughts to myself.

'Right. We've got a chance to do ourselves a bit of good, here.' Neither Bell nor I have ever heard Sculthorpe come out with so many words in one go.

'You mean, scarper back home?'

'Up your arse!'

'Ah, that's better. Why didn't you make yourself clear in the first place?'

'I mean winning the prize. We've got a great chance. Where's the map?'

'I thought you might be thinking about those two birds we saw.'

'Bugger the birds!'

'He's single minded, isn't he?'

'Stop messing about. I don't care what you two do. I'm taking this seriously. This counts towards The Best Recruit Competition, you know.'

'Blimey. I never realised that. That makes all the difference, doesn't it?'

'Oh, shut up and give us the map.' We hand it over obediently and watch while Sculthorpe struggles to unfold it. 'Now where are we?'

'Turn it up the other way and I'll try and tell you. What does that signpost say? Oh, yes. We must be about here. Between Titlington St Clements and Titlington Nethergate.'

'How far is that from the camp?'

'About six miles.'

'We'd better get a move on, then. Which way do we go?'

'He'd be in dead schtuck if he was on his own, wouldn't he?' says Bell as we traipse after the eager Sculthorpe.

'Yeah.' Bell and I gaze at each other thoughtfully. 'He couldn't fold that bleeding map up, let alone read it.'

'Gives me an idea,' says Bell. 'Here, hang on a minute, Sculthorpe.' Bell studies the map and shakes his head. Sculthorpe pads up and watches his face like a dog hearing the word 'walkies'.

'What is it?'

'I thought there might be a short cut here but it's probably easier to stick to the main road.' He points to a signpost saying 'Public Footpath. Fawcett Parva 3½ miles.' A glance at the map shows that Fawcett Parva is in exactly the opposite direction to the camp.

'Bugger it being easy. Is it going to be quicker?'

Bell shakes his head and turns to me. 'Difficult to say. It looks a bit tough to begin with.'

This is no exaggeration. The signpost points along a hedgerow choked with brambles and man-eating thistles. The last person to use it was probably the bloke who discovered Fawcett Parva.

'Saves about two miles as the crow flies,' I say helpfully.

'About that,' echoes Bell.

'What are we waiting for, then?' Sculthorpe is practically over the stile.

'I dunno,' says Bell doubtfully. 'I think, maybe, it would be safer to stick to the road.'

'You two twits can stick to the road. I want to win that prize.' Sculthorpe vaults off the stile and plunges into the undergrowth.

'And he was never seen again,' murmurs Bell. 'A few more like him and the Ruskies would chuck it in tomorrow.'

'He's keen, isn't he? I wonder whether they'll be able to give him directions in Liverpool.'

'I don't care much either way. Let's go and check out those birds.'

We toddle off down the road and are soon greeted by a sight to warm any nature lover's heart. Two cracking bints tightening their guy ropes. As I look over the hedge and watch their short shorts clinging jealously to their swelling haunches I marvel at the powers of recovery of the human body. A few days before I would not have thought it possible for Percy to make a dent in a custard pudding without being given the kiss of life first. I would rather have curled up with an album of Edward G. Robinson's baby photographs. Now, miraculously, I can look upon the female form without suffering an attack of instant nausea.

'Which one do you fancy?' says Bell.

'From this distance I'm not fussy.'

Bell runs his fingers through where his hair used to be and folds up the sleeves of his thick, khaki shirt.

'How do I look?'

'Fantastic. Those sweat patches under your armpits really do something for you.'

'Belt up. You ain't no bleeding Roger Moore in those trousers. You look like part of a Russian circus act.'

'Let's face it. Neither of us is going to start getting fan letters from Norman Hartnell. We'll have to rely on our charm, won't we?'

'Maybe the glamour of the uniform will see us through.'

'Like a dose of salts, I hope. Right, eyes down for the count up.' I vault nimbly over the fence and am grateful that the girls do not hear me when I land in a large cow pat. There is no doubt that we make a pathetic sight as we trundle through the long grass. When I think of what a natty dresser I was back in my Clapham days I could weep. I used to look a bleeding poem standing by the bandstand and taking the piss out of the middle-aged wankers going to sail their model yachts on the boating lake. Many a bird caught a catch in her throat and a catch in her tights in the same evening.

'Hello there. You all right, are you?' Bell's approach isn't going to give Cary Grant sleepless nights but it is slightly better than shoving your old man into a bird's hands and bursting into tears.

'Ooh, look, Noreen, it's the Army.' The bird on her hands and knees turns round so that I can have a butchers down her blouse. Very nice, too. 'We're not trespassing are we?'

'No. We were just passing through on an exercise and we wondered if you needed any help.'

'It's very kind of you,' says Noreen. 'We're not very good at this kind of thing. We've never done it before.'

'I wish we'd never done it at all,' says the other bird. 'This is the first day it hasn't rained.'

Bell nods towards the tent. 'You want to stone martin your spatlocks,' he says like his best friends call him Sherpa. 'These binions are a bit snaggled.'

'Almost spatulated,' I say, introducing a definite note of warning.

The blonde bird with the big knockers looks suitably impressed.

'Ooh, Noreen. Aren't we lucky to have fallen into the hands of The Professionals?'

My heart swells with pride as I hear the name of our advertising gimmick being repeated to me. It is not the only thing swelling, either. Beneath my drawers cellular, green, the mighty wurlitzer starts pumping himself up for yet another chorus of 'Love's old sweet melody'.

But, how, I begin to ask myself, can this natural desire to help others be translated into a sub-canvas nooky carnival? Fortunately Tinker Bell is equal to the challenge.

'You caught up with these two particular Professionals just in time,' he says grimly.

'What do you mean?' Both birds catch the slight hint of tension in his voice.

'Camborneo.'

'Camborneo?'

'In the Far East. There's a war been going on there for twenty-seven years.'

'I've never heard of it.'

Bell smiles wryly. 'Few people have. It's a dirty business. Not official. Communist infiltration. Dense jungle. Treaty obligation.'

'Top secret,' I say, seeing that he is drying up.

'It's going to be a bit different to this, isn't it?' Bell takes a deep breath and gazes across the surrounding fields like he was born and bred in one of them – if you saw him eating peas off the edge of his knife you would think he was.

'You're going there?'

I nod. 'Night parachute drop. Could be sticky. All those bamboos.'

'Ooh. You poor things.'

'It's a job. Just like any other.'

'Somebody's got to do it.' Blimey, if somebody started playing Greensleeves I think I would burst into tears.

'We came out for a last look around. I mean, last before we go, of course. England's not a bad place really, is it?'

'Funny how you never notice it till it's too late.' We both gaze along the row of electric pylons towards the municipal sewage works and a lump comes to the front of my trousers. Well, Noreen's mate has very humpty dumplings, if you know what I mean. She also wears an expression which says 'I want to help' more clearly than the photographs outside a massage parlour.

'I know just how you feel,' she says. I wish I could say the same about her, but who knows what time will bring? 'I felt awful when we went to the Isle of Man. But that's not quite the same, is it?' I don't think she expects an answer to that one so I drop to my knees and start tightening the guy ropes.

'Might as well see you all right before we go.'

'You are kind. You must have so much on your mind?'

'That's why it's a pleasure to do this,' I say. 'It helps take my mind off – off the other things. There, that's better.' I give one of the guy ropes a professional tweak. 'You never want to have too much hemispherical tension on your cross-plants.'

'Thank you so much.' She is practically wringing her hands with gratitude. 'Won't you stay and have a cup of tea before you go? It won't take us long to get the primus going.'

'That would be nice,' says Bell sincerely. 'I reckon we got the time, don't you, Timmy?'

'Yeah. We don't have to pick up our parachutes till eighteen hundred hours, do we?'

'I hope they work a bit better than Shorty Hardcastle's.'

' "Shorty Hardcastle"? Who's he?'

'He used to be Lofty Hardcastle until his 'chute failed to open.'

Noreen dashes a hand to her cake hole.

'How horrible!'

'Yeah. Let's talk about something more cheerful. It's funny—' Bell pauses dramatically. 'This countryside reminds me of when I was engaged. We went on a picnic once. I can see it as if it was only yesterday.'

'What happened?' says Noreen sympathetically.

'It ended. You couldn't blame her really. She never knew I was going to escape.'

'Escape?'

'Yeah, from this labour camp in Siberia. The coldest place on earth. I stole a couple of tennis rackets and tied them on my feet for snow shoes. Of course it was my own fault for being caught. My false red beard came off in a sauna behind Red Square. I remember—'

'Yeah, yeah,' I say hurriedly. 'Steady on, Tinker. Remember that's classified information and it hasn't been permed yet.' I mean! Tennis rackets in Siberia! The daft twit is getting carried away, isn't he? These birds are coming along very nicely without him overdoing it.

'She left you, did she?'

'She went off with someone else. They were setting up the banns when I came out of hospital. The frost bite.'

'Didn't have any lasting effects though, did it?' I move in fast again.

'That's terrible,' says Noreen's mate. 'How could a girl do that to any fellow? Didn't she even write?'

'She might have done. I never received a letter the whole time I was there.'

'No red letter days,' I say wittily.

Noreen looks at me coldly. 'I don't think it's anything to make jokes about.'

'Sometimes, if you didn't laugh you'd cry,' I rebuke her gently. Bell nods understandingly. 'Well, it's nice to have the company of a couple of attractive girls for our last few hours in Blighty, isn't it?'

'Very nice. It'll give us something to think about during the mongoose.'

'Don't you mean the monsoon?' says Noreen.

'That as well,' says Bell.

'Do you fancy a biscuit?' says Noreen's mate. 'They're a bit soggy but quite nice.'

Half an hour later we have discovered that Noreen's mate is called Veronica and that they both come from Birmingham and always go on holidays together.

'We don't like the same kind of fellows so we don't get in each other's hair,' explains Veronica.

Bell and I exchange glances and he gives me a crafty thumbs-up sign.

'You don't get a lot of blokes out here, do you?'

'You can say that again,' says Noreen bitterly. 'We went in a pub the other night and everybody stopped talking, like we was ghosts or something.'

'One fellow nearly swallowed his domino,' says Veronica. 'I think it was her leopard skin hot pants.'

'Well, you like to dress up a bit in the evenings, don't you?' says the aggrieved Noreen. 'I don't think we'll do this again. It was only because we got lent all the equipment, this time.'

'It's not a very big tent, is it?' I say, giving airspace to one of the things that has been worrying me. I mean, after my experience with the physical W.R.A.C.s I am dead keen that Percy should be tried in camera. (This is a legal reference and does not mean that I reckon on shoving my old man through the aperture of a Kodak Instamatic.)

'We've got another one. But we haven't had time to put it up, yet.'

There must be an answer to that, mustn't there? Thank goodness I am too refined to come out with it.

'We'll give you a hand,' I hear myself saying. 'Then you'll have more room to slip into your hot pants.' Bell closes his eyes and gives a little shudder of ecstasy.

'We couldn't ask you to do that,' says nice Noreen. 'We've been too much of an imposition already.'

'Think nothing of it. Like we said: you're helping us keep our minds off that moment when the plane door slides open and, there, thousands of feet below us, is the steaming jungle.'

'Well, if you're sure?'

'Positive,' I snake after Veronica and retrieve something that looks like a pile of dirty washing.

'We couldn't make head nor tail of it,' says Noreen. 'I don't expect it will take you thirty seconds.'

In fact it takes me fifteen seconds – to find out that I can't make head nor tail of it either. Veronica looks at me expectantly and I wonder what to do. She expects so much of me and that is just what I want to give her.

'We need a couple of poles,' I say, deciding on an instant change of tactic. 'Have you got a – an axe?' I am going to say chopper but it doesn't sound quite nice, does it?

'We've only got a bread knife.'

'That'll do,' I say hurriedly. I mean I am going to be an old man before I get anywhere at this rate. I cast my mince pies around and they light upon a convenient clump of trees. 'We should be able to get something out of that lot,' I say briskly. 'Where's that knife?'

Veronica ducks down and scrambles into her tent and I have to bite my lip. She has more curves than a Scalectrix track.

'It's a bit blunt,' she says.

'Don't worry. We'll manage.'

'You need a hand?' says Tinker casually.

'No. You stay here and get this lot untangled. I think the bittles have splayed.'

'Nasty.'

Veronica is practically scampering towards the wood and I sense that her obvious eagerness to help get the tent up is just the tip of the iceberg. She wants to do all she can to make my last few hours in the old country as pleasant as possible and I have no intention of standing in her way. I help her over the hedge and feel her firm young body slide down mine.

'You're strong, aren't you?' she murmurs approvingly.

'It's the life. When you're diving in and out of aeroplanes all the time you don't have much alternative.'

'Funny us meeting like this. Tomorrow you'll be thousands of miles away and we may never see each other again. Can I write to you?'

'Not where I'm going. There isn't even space for a bloke to run through the jungle with a forked stick.' I glance back towards the camp and see that Bell has got the tent spread out and is crawling under it. 'I think this will do,' I say, grabbing a handy sapling. 'You hold it down and I'll try and saw through it.' I sink to my haunches and lovely Veronica joins me, resting her peerless boobs on the bent sapling. We are facing each other and I allow myself a couple of to and fros with the bread knife before pausing to gaze into her large blue eyes. 'It might have been so different, mightn't it?' I say. Such remarks, though totally meaningless, always go down well with birds who can turn them into fodder for their restless imaginations.

'Yes,' she says. I hold her glance a few seconds more and then lean forward to kiss her gently on the lips. THWACK!! The daft bird lets go of the sapling and I get it smack in the kisser. If it had not ruckled her knockers first it could have been very nasty. I flop back and raise my hands to my afflicted mush, letting out a few words not usually found scrawled on vestry walls.

'Oh, no. Are you all right?' I peer through my fingers to see the mobile knocker factory towering over me. 'You don't want to injure yourself before you even get there.'

These are precisely my own thoughts and I permit myself a low groan such as might emit from the throat of a wounded leveret.

'How about you?' I say. 'It caught you a nasty one didn't it?' Without waiting for the shrill sound of an ambulance I apply my sensitive fingers to the wounded part and squeeze gently. 'No bones broken,' I observe and draw the bird down for a searching examination of my lip surfaces. Her own articles are soft as enzyme-tenderised marshmallows and fall upon my north and south like honeyed raindrops.

'That's better,' I murmur and there is no indication that she is going to disagree with me. My supple fingers find it easy to slip up under her halter necked blouse and I tug at her breasts like they are heavy foxgloves. She settles her whole weight on top of me and my hands are forced to close over her curvy back. I start fumbling for the catch of her shorts and she swiftly disentangles one of the hands that is ruffling the remains of my hair and snaps open a button and zip. Such an action on her part makes it easy for me to decide that her plans for the next few minutes are not a million miles away from my own and I greedily tug down her shorts leaving her pants ruckled fetchingly across the twin peaks of her back buffers. Percy is now surging against the serge and beginning to lift Veronica into the air like a car jack. Ever mindful of the welfare of man's best friend I ease outdoor girl onto her back and thoughtfully arrange her shorts under her backside before completing the removal of her panties – little things like that mean a lot to a woman. I lend my right hand to her spasm chasm and we trade lips whilst I try to remove my boots and gaiters. This is a darn sight more difficult than it should be and the bloke who designed the Army uniform should be censored for lack of imagination. If you have ever tried to slip out of a pair of size ten Army boots you will know what I mean. In the end I have to withdraw my fingers from their furry friend and concentrate on untangling the strips of leather that the Army gives you instead of boot laces.

Such an act might well have broken the spell that surrounds our amorous dalliance but Veronica is not a girl who lies there and makes a shopping list on the ceiling. While I toil, her eager fingers flip open my flies and disappear into my drawers cellular like jackrabbits into a cornfield. Percy springs forward eagerly to greet his visitors and there is a touching reunion that might well bring tears to my thighs if I did not keep firm – and I mean firm – control of myself.

'It's hot, isn't it?' murmurs Veronica. She may well be referring to the weather but I doubt it. 'If I can't write to you I might as well give you something to remember me by.' She lowers her head and brushes her cheek against the source of many of my problems before embarking on a full-scale taste test. What she is doing straightens me out like I was pegged up to dry, and in the end it is she who removes my boots and gaiters and tugs my trousers over my heels. And all the time she does not say a word. Just finds room at the back of her throat for a few growls. She sounds like a moggy warning another cat to stay away from its milk.

By the time she has finished, Percy is more highly tuned than a speed fiend's dragster – and practically making revving noises as well. I flip Veronica onto her back and the old man takes off like he is trying to break some kind of world speed record. I had been contemplating a friendly muff dive but in his present mood my action man kit is going to nudge any contender in a race for the furry doughnut.

'G-r-r-r-gh!' says my new friend. 'G-G-rrgh!!' She grabs hold of me like she thinks I am in danger of falling off a window ledge and lets out a noise like a rattlesnake's gargling competition. What a performer this bird is. Talk about uncontrolled! She makes Shirley Bassey seem like Julie Andrews on a Brownies' outing. It is as well that she is breaking up like a wafer factory in a tornado because my powers of control are evaporating faster than spit on a griddle. I try and think about Sir Alf Ramsey but it is no good. Soft currents of electric lust ripple through my loins and I find myself paddling faster and faster to keep up with the flood.

'I wouldn't do this unless you were going away,' she says, 'Oh!! Oh! Oh! OH!!'

With the thunderous roar of a million hooves behind us we hurtle past the winning post in a dead heat and I suck in great mouthfuls of air and a bluebottle. The bird is still trembling and there is a pleasing smile etched across her mug. 'That was fabulous,' she murmurs. 'You are clever.'

I do not say anything because I am trying to get rid of the bluebottle without spitting it over her shoulder. You may ask why I should bother with such delicacies but I am like that. One of the old school.

Five minutes later we are wending our way back to the camp. The second tent is still flat but there is a considerable amount of movement coming from beneath it. Bell and Noreen cannot be seen but as we approach the heaving canvas there is a long-drawn-out sigh and the movement stops.

'You haven't got it up yet, have you?' I say, immediately regretting my choice of words.

'You wanna bet?' says a muffled voice from the tent. A few seconds later Bell's legs protrude from the canvas and these, fortunately, are still connected to the rest of his body and capable of supporting it. 'I thought it might be easier to do it from the inside,' he says.

'Original, certainly,' I say. 'How did you get on?'

'I found where the poles go. Did you get any?'

'No, the knife was too blunt.'

'Oh, well that's the end of that then, isn't it? You girls will have to make do with the one you've got.'

It does not escape my notice that Tinker Bell's desire to help has wilted faster than a beerlogged prick at a brewery outing.

Noreen emerges from beneath the canvas looking flushed and I observe that she has her shorts on back to front. Obviously, a good time has been had by all.

'Better be getting back to the Ops Room,' I say, allowing my stiff upper lip to tremble in the slight breeze .'We can't afford to be late for this one.' I turn to Veronica who is either crying or has something in her eye. 'Thanks for – for everything.'

'Good luck. Take care of yourselves.'

'We'll do our best, eh Timmy?'

I nod and for some reason find myself limping as we walk towards the road. Maybe it was because I saw 'The Dam Busters' seven times when I was a kid.

'What a smashing couple of birds,' says Bell as we start scampering down the road. 'How soon do you think we can get back there?'

'What are you talking about? We're dropping behind enemy lines tonight, remember?'

'We could say there'd been a change of plan.'

'Don't be daft. After all that bullshit you gave them you'd have to go back with your head in a sling before they'd give you the time of day. Don't you understand? They were doing that for England. It was one of those bitter sweet memories of war that will stay with them all their lives. Don't you ever go to the pictures? I thought the way you were going on you knew what you were doing.'

Bell smiles to himself. 'It was all right though, wasn't it? I wouldn't mind going overseas for real if I could have a bit of that before I went.'

'Don't let the War Office hear you say that. Anyway, we're not going to go anywhere unless we can get back to camp double quick. At this rate Sculthorpe will be there before us.'

But Sculthorpe is not there before us. We see him staggering along beside the main road as we speed past in the back of a lorry. He is glistening with sweat and there are so many burrs over his uniform that it looks as if he has tried to camouflage himself. He does not recognise us which is probably a good thing.

CHAPTER FIVE

Sculthorpe gets put on a charge for coming in last of the whole company and stops being Sergeant Lake's blue-eyed boy at exactly the same instant.

'You boogers!' he wails. 'You set me up. You wanted me to lose myself.'

'If you'll excuse the expression: bollocks!' says Bell firmly. 'It's not our fault we can't read maps. We didn't get in much before you, remember. We just made a mistake, that's all.'

'We were telling you not to go that way,' I say. 'You should have read the map for yourself.'

'I'm sorry about the bull,' says Bell. 'But look on the bright side. It's a clean wound and lots of blokes have to go to Spain before they get the chance to be gored.'

'Nobody's going to be able to see it. Except your best friend – if you ever have one,' I chip in.

'Up your arse!'

'Exactly!' we chorus.

After four weeks of bullying my boots until I could use them to look up girls' skirts, and learning so much regimental history that I start repeating The Loamshire's battle honours in my sleep, I – in company with the rest of the intake – am informed that I will be allowed to go down to the local town on Saturday afternoon. The news is received with the kind of enthusiasm that would accompany the issue of free season tickets to the 'Wet Dream Festival'. Every pimple factory in the billet starts talking as if Sophia Loren will be waiting for him outside the chemist's and the sight of them all running their bug rakes through the goosegog fluff on top of their nuts is calculated to make strong men weep.

Not, of course, that I intend to deny the local populace

the opportunity to see Clapham's answer to Douglas Fairbanks Junior. It is just that I don't reckon on coming back with love bites all over my action man kit – unless they have forgotten to fumigate the local flea pit.

'What do you reckon on doing?' says Bell as we arrange our cap badges squarely over our left eyes and prepare to report to the guardroom to see if we are in a fit state to be unleashed on the British public – there is absolutely no chance of anyone being allowed out in civvies.

'I don't know, I reckon a tea dance, then I might do my Rudolph Valentino impression.'

'Come off it.'

'I don't know. Get pissed I suppose.'

'We've got to be back in camp before opening time.'

'Oh, bleeding heck. I'll open an artery and lie in the gutter. How does that grab you?'

'There must be some birds about.'

'Yeah. I can imagine. I bet the only time they take the straws out of their mouths is when it's milking time and they're tickling the cows' udders. Even if there is something half-way decent it'll be fixed up by the time we get there.'

When we have eventually satisfied the R.M.P.s that the studs on the bottoms of our boots are correctly arranged to print the regulation pattern on dog shit, the last of the lorries has left the camp and we are forced to try and hitch a lift. We are having no luck and are on the point of chucking it in and returning to have an uninterrupted run at the N.A.A.F.I. pin table when a little Italian Fart spins round the corner. Behind the wheel is curvy Miss Bientot. I leap into the road and she nearly runs up my instep before stopping.

'Could you give us a lift, Miss Bientot?' I whine. 'We missed the transport.'

'Rosemurch,' she says. Can't be bad can it? First name terms already. 'It'll be a tight squeeze,' she continues. 'You'd better climb in through the roof. Where are you going?'

'Nowhere in particular. Just down town to have a look round.'

I don't know what perfume she is using but it doesn't take many prisoners. The car is so small that it seems like a kind of see-through bra for her enormous tits.

'I'm going to the garden party at the vicarage.' She waits expectantly but both Bell and I manage to control ourselves. 'It's open to the public.'

'We might pop in later, mightn't we?' I say to Bell. I mean, the Devil must have other work for idle hands, mustn't he?

'It's a very good cause. And talking of popping in, I haven't seen either of you at the library, have I?'

'We haven't had a moment, so far.'

'Don't leave it too long. You can't beat a good read, you know.'

'She's not bad, is she?' says Bell as we watch the small marvel of Italian workmanship frog-farting round the corner. 'I reckon behind that posh voice she would quite fancy a bit.'

'I reckon she would fancy a bit behind anything. Why don't you nip round to the vicar's knees-up and ask her?'

'I don't fancy the setting. Come on, let's find out where the action is.'

The depressing thing about Westery – or, more exactly, one of the many depressing things about Westery – is that it is full of berks exactly like ourselves. All of them looking for a good time that exists only in their imaginations. All of them looking as if they put on each other's uniforms by mistake. One bloke who is with a bird has a smile zooming away from both sides of his cake hole like it is trying to meet round the back of his nut.

'I didn't fancy her,' says Bell.

'Diabolical. It's just like what I said. Load of rubbish. I couldn't be seen dead with that. I'd rather go without.'

'Me, too. It's sad that blokes have to stoop so low.'

'Well, we don't.'

'Of course not. Look at that one, for instance. I just couldn't bring myself to do it.'

'Not in a million years. If she was the only bird in the world I wouldn't go near her.'

'You wouldn't be able to get near her.'

'You know what I mean – oh, hello – I mean, good afternoon!' We are passing the Blue Boar when out trips lovely Amanda Nasty. She is wearing a light summer frock and a perplexed expression which gets more perplexed as she looks at me. 'I don't think—'

'We had the pleasure on the train,' I remind her. I didn't mean to put it like that but these things slip out sometimes, don't they?

'Oh yes. I didn't recognise you with your hair cut.' She looks nervously over her shoulder as Lieutenant Bland appears. He is wearing a hacking jacket and an expression that could get him seeded in the 'Upper Class Twit Of The Year' competition. 'We're going to the point-to-point,' she explains. 'I do hope you're enjoying everything.' With these words and a light wave she seizes Bland's arm and they disappear through an archway towards the car park. 'Barmy' acknowledges our salute by tapping his forehead with one finger as if conceding that he is round the twist.

'She could barely keep her hands off you, could she?' sneers Bell. 'I've seen some brush-offs in my time—'

'Mostly from dead in front of your eyes I should reckon. Lay off me, will you? If I told you half of what that bird and I got up to you wouldn't believe me.'

'If you told me a quarter I wouldn't believe you. Off to the point-to-point, eh? There's posh for you.'

'Do you reckon? My Mum always said it was rude to point-to-point.'

'Oh blimey! Your jokes. I can't take any more. I'm going back to camp.'

I have half a mind – watch it! – to follow him when a shifty-looking geezer shoves a piece of paper in my hand. I am on the point of throwing it away – well, you don't know where it's been, do you? – when I see that it is headed 'Free Sex'. Such a headline grabs me tighter than a pair of boy scout's Y-fronts and I read on. 'Adult entertainment for Britain's fighting men. The show that drove the N.A.A.F.I. daffy; that E.N.S.A. tried to censor. Tita Lotof invites you to share the intimate atmosphere of "The Club on Wheels", Europe's most frank and open temple of sexual freedom. Thrill to the titillating striptease of Nora "My Body Is My Life" Nibbler, the exotic illusions of Trixie "Where's the banana?" Bigun. This super stag show has been specially assembled for the men with their fingers on the trigger. Membership and entrance only 50p. No dogs.' Underneath this exciting information is stamped 'Cowslip Lane. 1500–2200 hours'.

'Funny place to have it,' says Bell who is looking over my shoulder.

'Yeah. Might be a giggle though, mightn't it?' Of course that kind of thing leaves me colder than a mermaid's quim but I am not above going along for a laugh. It amuses me to watch the audience, if you know what I mean.

'Can't be worse than this lot.' We watch another lucky soldier boy stroll by with his arm almost round the broad back of a bird built like a badly lagged boiler.

A hill rises sharply behind the church and we are told that Cowslip Lane is a turning off the road running up to it. It is not difficult to believe that one is travelling in the right direction because a steady stream of khaki covered enthusiasts is beginning to choke the highway.

'There must be a few bob in this caper,' says Bell. 'It's probably why they can keep the price down. Ah, there's the paybox.' We can see a large caravan with a cluster of blokes round it and I wonder where the club is. Surely they don't use a tent?

'All right, lads. Let the hot dog see the rarebit. Keep away from the entrance, please. You'll all get a dekko, don't you worry.'

The geezer with the straw hat and the megaphone is not unknown to me.

'Sidney!'

My brother-in-law nearly goes into orbit. 'Timmy! Blimey, don't ever do that to me again. I've got a weak heart, you know.'

I take a closer look at the caravan and realise that it is not sharing the landscape with anything. The back is open and a crowd of blokes are straining forward to get a butchers at what is going on inside. It dawns on me that this must be 'The Club On Wheels'. I can understand why they call the atmosphere 'intimate'.

'Is this it, Sidney?' I say. 'Are you something to do with this? What happened to the hula hoops?'

Sidney looks round carefully and drapes his arm across my shoulder. When Sidney does that most people feel as secure as a turkey having its tummy tickled at Christmas time.

'Come and have a chat,' he says. 'I'm glad to see you, I really am. Mum lost your address.'

'Typical.'

'She wrote it on the back of a TV Times Dad tore up for the khasi.'

'Very symbolic.'

'That's what I said. I said "That's a blooming symbolic thing to do, Dad." '

'And what did he say?'

'He said, "Symbolics to you and all, mate." Dirty old sod.'

'This is my mate, Tinker Bell,' I say, deciding that I can exist without too many reminders of home.

'Pleased to meet you, Tinker. Any friend of Timmy's is a friend of mine.'

'Let that be a warning to you,' I say. 'Come on, Sid. What happened with the hula hoops?'

Sidney leads us away and shouts at a bloke with a face like a crazy dachshund to look after things.

'Not hula hoops, pogo sticks. I had a bit of bad luck, didn't I?'

'What happened, Sid?'

'Bleeding springs went after half a dozen jumps. I had to reverse the pedals and job the lot off as non-collapsible shooting sticks. They're very popular in Japan, you know.'

'I didn't know that, Sidney.'

'Oh yes. They buy more copies of *Country Life* than you've had hot dinners. There's not many Japanese families that don't have a pair of plus fours tucked away behind their ancestor's relics.'

'How did you get into show business, Sid?'

'Well, you know I've always had a ponce on.'

'That's news to me, Sid. I always thought you were straight.'

'What are you rabbiting about?! Of course I'm straight. Can't you speak English? "Ponce on" means you fancy something.'

'That's penchant, you berk.' Sidney always gets his new words from the *Reader's Digests* he looks at while waiting to get his medical certificates for sickness benefit, so he has to work out the pronunciation for himself.

'Oh, bugger it. I don't care what it is. You know what I mean. I was in films, wasn't I? And I ran that club in the West End. I'm practically Mr Show Business.'

'That's why you went into hula hoops?'

'Don't take the piss, Timmy. I found that show business didn't give me the emotional satisfaction I need. It's a very cut-throat business, Timmy. Very dog eat dog. That's why I was so responsive to Vasco's idea.'

'Vasco?'

'Vasco Snippet. My partner.' Sid indicates the mean-featured geezer who is currently extracting 50p's from the wave of khaki breaking against the back of the caravan. 'He pointed it all out to me. What we're doing at the moment is fulfilling a social need as well as making a few bob. You know what the War Office are like?'

'Not actually, Sid, no.'

'Well they're out of touch. The fighting man of today wants adult entertainment. It's no good giving him fat old sopranos and blokes bringing rabbits out of hats. You wouldn't take it in civvy street so why have it here? You know better than I do what these blokes want. Cooped up all day without any female company, bromide instead of sugar. I reckon it's in the Army's interest to keep them on their toes. I tried to get the War Office to give us a subsidy, like the Arts Council, but they didn't want to know. Diabolical, that's what I call it.'

'Definitely, Sid.'

'But I wasn't taking no for an answer. With Vasco's help I formed "The Club On Wheels" and we travel round the Army camps trying to bring a little fun and gaiety to the defenders of western civilisation.'

'Very praiseworthy, Sid.'

'Yeah. I think it's a very autistic venture.'

'Altruistic too, Sid.'

'Exactly, it's a bit of everything. Genuine artistry goes into this show. It's not a load of rubbish.'

'We'd like to have a look at it,' I say, trying to keep any trace of eagerness out of my voice.

'Be my guest,' says Sidney. 'Tell you what. Since you're family and you've got your mate with you, I'll let you both in for half price.'

'Blimey, Sid. Are you sure you can afford it?'

Sid shakes his head thoughtfully. 'Well, now you come to mention it, I suppose I shouldn't be giving away my partner's money, should I? O.K. that will be a quid for the two of you.'

'Tight as a gnome's french letter,' I murmur to Tinker as we push our way through the crowd of blokes fighting their way into the caravan. If blood is thicker than water you would need a colour test to tell the difference in our family.

'Nice view, isn't it,' says Bell. He nods down towards the church and the sprawling town giving way to green fields and hills in the background.

'Yeah, smashing. Makes me wish I'd brought my easel with me.'

The caravan is as long as a donkey's dongler and it needs to be. There is a curtain at the end and a low barrier in front of it to hold back the audience. Vasco's lips are moving as he snatches our 50p's and I imagine he is checking the size of the house. His flesh is kipper-coloured and he niffs a bit like one of our finny friends as well. Maybe it is the excitement. A crowd of blokes is surging in behind us and reluctantly Vasco spreads his arms as the caravan shudders.

'That's enough, boys. You wait for the next show, now.'

'We got in just in time,' says Bell.

I don't have time to reply before a bird comes through the curtain wearing a couple of tits that look like the back view of an elephant kneeling down to say its prayers. Tita Lotof, unless my mince pies deceive me. She is wearing a dress cut lower than Ted Heath's re-election prospects and is greeted by a chorus of whistles and sophisticated shouts of 'Get 'em orf!' and 'Drop 'em!'

'Thank you for that wonderful reception and welcome to "The Club On Wheels". First of all I would like to ask anyone who does not believe wholeheartedly in the principles of total sexual freedom to leave the club.' The pressure on the crush barrier becomes even greater and I begin to worry about the bloke standing behind me. It's his smile as much as anything.

'Good. I can see we are all of the same mind.' She undoes the halter at the back of her dress and the front two rows duck as an avalanche of flesh rolls towards them. She moves swiftly along the front row and the caravan trembles again as a forest of hands stretch out to feel the merchandise.

'That's good, that's good,' she breathes. 'I feel good vibrations.'

I am feeling some very bad vibrations and I turn round to tell the bloke behind me about it. Maybe it is not all his fault because a fresh wave of bodies are breaking past Vasco who seems more keen on extracting his 50p than stopping them. I haven't been in such a crush since Millicent Honeywood's mum and dad came home early and forced us to take refuge in the broom cupboard. I can still feel that ironing board burrowing into the small of my back.

'And now! The sensation of the Cannes Film Festival: Trixie Bigun!'

'She means the Canned Film Festival, does't she?' Tinker has a point there, as I have to admit when Trixie staggers onto the stage, belches and stumbles into the grateful audience. Whether she intended to shed the top half of her clothing it is impossible to say but by the time Tita has dragged her back on stage she is revealing a couple of perky tits turning up their noses like reversed hunting horns. She is a very long lady with legs that go all the way up to the tips of her ear rings.

'We are going to do a little play for you now entitled "The Case of the Missing Cucumber",' trills Tita and a ripple of anticipation runs through the audience. Unfortunately it coincides with the arrival of another inrush of bodies and I feel myself propelled towards the stage as a shout of alarm goes up. It might well not be the only thing going up, I think to myself but I do not have a lot of time to develop the thought. It is strange, but although the inrush of bodies has stopped we still seem to be moving forward. It takes me a couple of seconds to realise what has happened, and by that time I am flat on my face underneath a pile of bodies. The caravan has shaken free of its moorings and is rolling down the hill! The sound of undergrowth crashing against the side confirms my fears.

I don't know if you have ever rolled down a hill inside a caravan full of blokes and three naked birds but I can tell you that it is a very dangerous way to get your kicks. By the time the bleeding thing finally stops we have had more bodily contact than one and a half pounds of hamburger steak in a mincing machine. Why the thing didn't turn over I will never know. Quite where I end up I am too much of a gentleman to reveal but if you have ever chewed a dry Brillo pad you will get some idea.

'Get off me, you dirty monkey!' squeals the bint revealing that she has suffered no serious damage to the vocal chords.

'Fire!' screams another voice. I remove my head from between Nora 'My body is my life' Nibbler's legs and turn it with difficulty. Flames can indeed be seen leaping above the shoulders of those now fleeing through the back of the caravan. In such a situation it occurs to me that I would be foolish not to follow them and I start scrambling to my feet, much to the relief of Tinker Bell whose recent silence has been occasioned by my knee being wedged in his cake hole.

'Run for it!' I say, more to check that my own shout box is in good nick than because I reckon that he is going to start cataloguing his stamp collection. Nora and her mates are no slouches when it comes to pulling on the running shoes and the five of us hit daylight practically nipple to tit.

The sight that meets our eyes is unusual to put it mildly. Three vicars and half a dozen boy scouts, one of whom is holding a Union Jack. Bell must be concussed or something because he stops to salute the flag. There is a lot of bunting hanging about and it suddenly dawns on me that we have crashed the vicarage garden party. The fire must have been caused by the caravan coming to a stop in the middle of the barbecue pit. 'Where my caravan has roasted' as the song has it. I realise this when one of the squaddies runs past with a string of sausages round his neck.

'Keep moving, you berk!' I hiss at Bell and give him an encouraging boot up the backside.

With the arrival of Tita, Nora and Trixie the vicars' mugs turn a hideous shade of white and it is obvious that, though conditioned to the multiple sufferings of others, they have not yet come to terms with galloping nudity. A lot of old girls are bawling their nuts off and the sight of my mates doing a bunk through the vicar's hedge reminds me of a traffic jam at Beecher's Brook. The scene is a very embarrassing one for all concerned and I am not spared my share of suffering. As I turn to scarper I blunder into Miss Rosemurch A. Bientot who is standing with her arms full of coconuts – at least I think her arms are full of coconuts, with Miss R. A. B. it is difficult to be certain.

She gazes upon my torn and ruckled clothing and there is no doubt that she recognises my predicament.

CHAPTER SIX

'She didn't recognise me,' says Bell smugly.

'I'm not surprised with a string of sausages wrapped round your mug. We didn't all have the chance to camouflage ourselves.'

Tinker and I have limped back to camp listening to the chimes of the fire engine bells grow fainter in the distance.

'I never knew greenhouses could burn,' says Bell.

'Must have been something to do with the way it was heated.'

'Don't worry, I think they saved the house. Did you see Sidney?'

'Your brother-in-law? No, but I saw his mate. He was crawling about saying he was ruptured.'

'Must have fallen on his money belt. Blimey, but I'll always remember the expression on that Fire Escapee's face. His stiff white collar went all limp and soggy when he saw Nora.'

'I bet they shook up the Women's Institute tea tent when they bolted inside.'

'Stands to reason. Especially with Trixie's snake.'

'Snake?'

'Yeah. A blooming great python. I saw it chasing one of the boy scouts into the first aid tent.'

'Poor little sod.'

'It was probably just frightened. I don't reckon they eat when they're scared.'

'Well I do. Do you fancy one?' Bell feels inside his shirt and produces the remains of a string of sausages.

'Not raw, thanks.'

'All right, fussy. I'll go and put them on top of the boiler in the ablutions.'

He pads off leaving me to consider the latest load of trouble I have landed myself in. Miss A. Bientot – I wonder what the A. stands for – got a face-full of my features and could well put the finger on me had she a mind to. As we legged it away from the vicarage, M.P.s were beginning to roll up like bluebottles making for a cart-load of horse shit. Maybe I had better ramble round to the unit library and nobble her before the khaki fuzz get there. If I borrow the complete works of Shakespeare she may be prepared to turn a lenient eye on me.

I am also worried about Sidney. His caravan may be a possible source of charcoal but I reckon its days as 'Europe's most frank and open temple of sexual freedom' are well and truly over. Poor old Sid! He has not been having a lot of luck lately and I am prepared to bet that Vasco Snippet was putting up more inspiration than ackers. I wish there was something I could do but I am not allowed out of the camp until the following Saturday, and then only if my attendance at the vicarage garden party remains a secret. I must get round to Miss Bientot before she can start blabbing.

This is easier said than done because Major Nasty is having his first check-up on the intake's progress and this means that Lieutenant Bland is climbing on Sergeant Lake who is climbing on Corporal Martin and the whole bleeding lot of them are toppling over onto us. Bags of bull and bags of drill means that the only time I can get round to the unit library is when it is closed. I hear from a bloke in another intake that the M.P.s have been asking questions and a serious attack of panic sends clammy fingers running up and down my action man kit like they are trying to play a tune on it.

Eventually I manage to salvage half an hour when I should be rubbing soft circles of spit into my best boots and belt round to the unit library. It is strange, because it is the only place on the camp which does not shout Army at you. Only the notice board telling you what to do if you pick up a dose of the clap has a faintly martial ring about it.

Miss Bientot sits behind a desk reading. She is alone – that is unless there are a load of blokes kneeling down behind the filing cabinets. I cough discreetly and she looks up as if surprised to see anyone. Will she recognise me?

'Oh, it's you,' she says.

'Yes,' I say. I mean, I can hardly argue with her, can I?

'I've been thinking about you,' she says.

'Oh. yes?' She does not make it sound as if she has my photograph by the side of her bed.

'What should I do about you?' she says sternly. 'I have a responsibility, you know.'

'That's what I came to see you about,' I say.

Miss Bientot gets up, crosses to the door and looks out to see if there is anyone about. The hall is as empty as one of Twiggy's bra cups. She hangs up a notice saying 'Library Closed', closes the door and returns to me.

'Yes?'

'It's quite simple, really,' I blurt out. 'I was walking down the hill towards the fête when suddenly this caravan comes crashing through the hedge. I realised that it was out of control and that somebody could get hurt so I tried to stop it. I jumped on the back but it was gathering speed all the time and there was nothing I could do.'

'If you jumped on the back how was it that you were one of the last people to emerge?' Miss Bientot pulls down her cashmere sweater and her bristols swell forward like a couple of seals hearing the clink of the keeper's bucket.

'I pushed my way down the front to see if I could find any controls.'

'How very brave of you. You must be in the running for a medal. Trying to stop a runaway caravan. Does your platoon commander know about this?'

'No!' I squeal.

Miss Bientot purses her rich plum-red lips.

'Well, I think he ought to. Your modesty is very praiseworthy but it should not stand as a barrier between you and your just reward.'

'It wasn't only that,' I say hurriedly. 'I was a bit worried that some people might think I had been watching the show in Cowslip Lane.'

'Was that where the show was?' says Miss B. artfully.

'Somebody told me there was some kind of entertainment going on up there,' I say quickly. 'I think that's where all those girls came from.'

'They didn't join you in trying to stop the caravan?'

'I don't think so. Of course, I can't be certain. The whole thing is a bit confused.'

'It does seem confused,' agrees Miss B. 'Why are you telling me all this?'

'I didn't want you to get the wrong idea. I mean, you said at the beginning that you didn't know what to do about me.'

'Y-e-e-s.' Miss Bientot slowly tucks a bookmark into the margin of the page she is reading and closes the book with a snap. 'What are we going to do with you? Now that you've explained everything I can understand your desire to avoid publicity. But your bravery deserves some reward.'

'Perhaps I could take out an extra library book,' I say.

'Perhaps.' Miss Bientot rises to her feet and smoothes down her skirt. 'What kind of thing do you like? Travel? Fiction? Adventure?' When she says 'adventure' she gives a little shiver and I get the feeling that she may be interested in more than just stamping my library tickets. Certainly all that make-up she plasters over her mug must be there to attract someone.

'Or sport,' she says. 'Do you like playing games?'

'I'm interested in skiing,' I say.

'Ah, you like sheing.'

'I like that too.'

Miss Bientot gives a light laugh – or as light as a bird of

her not inconsiderable physique can manage. '"Sheing" is how the Norwegians pronounce what you call skiing. Norway is the home of sheing, you know.'

I did not know that but I don't feel that my life has been any the poorer for it. 'I joined up because I wanted to learn to ski,' I tell her.

Miss B. looks surprised. 'There must be easier ways,' she says. 'Now let me see. Sheing. We do have a book somewhere.' She runs her fingers along the rows of books on the shelves and shakes her head.

'Somebody must have taken it out.' She gives a little smile as if remembering something. 'Or perhaps it's in the stock room. I take them in there if they're looking poorly – torn covers, that kind of thing. Shall we have a look?'

I nod winsomely and pad after her through a door marked 'PRIVATE'. Somebody anxious to step into Noel Coward's shoes has added an S. There are piles of books everywhere, some of them new.

'Some of these books are allowed out to officers only. We try to avoid controversial subjects like sex being too widely distributed.' Miss Bientot shivers again.

'Naturally,' I say. 'The blokes can get enough of that up Cowslip Lane, can't they? What's this one, then?'

The book I have picked up is called *A History Of Flogging In The British Army*. 'Did the officers have a whip round for this one?' I say wittily.

Miss B. winces. 'That's Major Nasty. Officers are allowed to order books. He's very interested in corporal punishment.'

'I thought they were just good friends,' I say keeping the rib ticklers thundering in like Pacific breakers – or brakers as seems more clearly the case if I read the expression on Miss B.'s face correctly.

'You did say sheing, didn't you?' she says. 'It's not a subject we get a lot of demand for. Japanese martial arts are very popular at the moment. Does that appeal at all?'

'Not unless you can do it on skis.'

'You mustn't look at that one!' Miss B. snatches up a book I have not even glanced at.

'Why? What's it called? "How to desert and live happily ever after"?'

'No. It might give you ideas of a different type.' That perfume is beginning to work me over again and in the soft light the lady's boobs are looking a right tempting handful – and a left tempting handful as well; I don't have any favourites.

'Let's have a shufti.' The bint obviously wants me to see the book so I grab it from her unresisting fingers.

'You mustn't look.' She reminds me of Avril Pottersman taking off her knicks in the middle of Clapham Common when every bush down to the bandstand was alive with the crackle of plastic macs and she was flashing for all of them.

'*An Anthology of Eastern Love Arts*. Blimey, don't tell me Major Nasty ordered this as well?'

'No. It was Lieutenant Bland, actually.'

'Good grief! I didn't reckon him as being on page one of Western Love Arts let alone the Advanced Driving Course.'

'Perhaps he's trying to broaden his repertoire,' says Miss B. coyly.

'I didn't think there was anything you could do about that,' I say. I mean, even the sex shop catalogues don't promise you that, do they? I can't see the point of bothering, myself. Be thankful for what you've got is my motto.

Miss Bientot blushes. 'You must give it back. Some of those illustrations . . .' Her voice tails away as if unable to cope with what its owner has seen.

Dutifully, I open the book and – Blimey! 'He's got a broad repertoire, hasn't he? Long as well.'

'Some of those temple carvings are quite obscene,' pants Miss B. 'There's one on page—' She corrects herself. 'Some of them are too disgusting to think about.'

I have a quick skim through the book and by the time I have finished the room is about ten degrees hotter. I soon get bored with dirty pictures – about three hours after I have started looking at them as a rule – but these are very artistic and to a bloke of my sensitive nature that makes all the difference. I mean, none of the geezers in them have any socks on for a start. I remember how our little Nippon mates used to use filthy folios to get them in the right mood for a flesh fest and they certainly had a point.

'They're awful, aren't they?' breathes Miss B. at my elbow. 'That one there. I shouldn't think it's physically possible.'

'You probably have to be very supple,' I agree with her.

'I'd better tuck it away before it falls into the wrong hands.' She is referring to the book as I discover when she withdraws it from my fingers and turns to the shelves. 'I'll pop it up here out of harm's way.' She approaches a rickety step ladder and shins up it, giving me another chance to case her joints. At the top she cocks one leg behind her in the classic 'I was never missed before' pose and turns to me as the ladder starts to wobble. I spring forward to her assistance, catch my foot in the lamp flex and, as the room is plunged into darkness, Miss Bientot plunges into my arms. Terrible, isn't it? There might have been a nasty accident. Fortunately my Garth-like physique is equal to the strain and I sink to the floor where I am in the enviable position of being the only thing between it and Miss Bientot.

'Are you all right?' she says. Not entirely to my surprise I hear her voice speaking from a position approximately half an inch from my lips and the pong of her perfume is leaving no room in my hooter for anything else.

'Yeah,' I breathe and allow my lips to blunder into hers. If she is furious about this she has a funny way of showing it because her mouth anchors itself securely to mine and her enormous bristols pile up against my chest like two sheep huddling against a cliff face.

'You're wicked,' she murmurs eventually. 'I should never have let you look at that book.'

I have to confess that, though a bit on the plump side

with the lights on, Miss B. becomes a curve carnival once you start tapping out love's old sweet song in the warm darkness.

'I shouldn't let you do this,' she says grabbing the inside of my thigh like she is playing 'Hunt The Truncheon'. 'I expect you want me to do all those naughty things you saw in that book?'

'Not all of them,' I say desperately. I mean! Harm can come to a young boy like that. I don't mind trying something a bit different but Percy has not got any friends with him and some of those positions need a cast of thousands.

'I mustn't spoil my dress.' Miss B. sits up and briskly begins to remove her clothes. I can see her body silhouetted agains the light that comes through a ventilation grille and the whole scene is like a do-it-yourself blue movie. Off comes her bra and the mighty knockers lunge forward as if they have been let off a lead. Her dress has been unzipped and hangs round her waist so I help her wriggle out of it and run my fingers lightly over her stomach as she bends forward to toss it onto the table. My hand flicks into the top of her panties and as she lies back I slide it down to feel her minge fringe. I coil my fingers in the tight curls and then let them explore on into happy valley.

'Take your uniform off!' Miss Bientot's tone would be a credit to Sergeant Lake. It's funny how birds can be so coy and then, suddenly—

'Ouch! Watch it!' I yelp. 'You'll spoil the set.' Miss B. does not look the kind of bird who spent her formative years on a potato farm but you can never tell. The way she is mauling Percy you would think he was seven pounds of King Edwards.

'I want you,' she says. This is no surprise to the front of my trousers and it is a good job that the War Office make things to last.

'Hold on a minute,' I tell her, 'I'm not going anywhere.' I struggle out of my boots, gaiters and trousers while Miss

Bientot tries to lose her tongue in my earhole. Really this bird is more worked up than Sid when he paid a couple of quid to see a passion play and found it was all about religion.

'Fabulous,' she drools as her fingers close about the not unwilling Percy.

'Not so tight!' I squeal. By the cringe, this bird must have been a devil for the plasticine when she was a kid. She squeezes my action man kit like it is the fag end of a tube of toothpaste.

'Grrrrrrgh!' Now she is sliding down my body and Percy suddenly finds himself in a cleft tit. She waggles herself backwards and forwards and then continues her journey to guzzle terminus. I am amazed that I can't see the purple python glowing in the darkness as I quiver with anticipatory excitement.

'He's a naughty boy,' she scolds.

'Get on with it!' I feel like shouting, but birds are always like that when they have you at their mercy.

I stretch out my hand and try to feel for her spasm chasm but she nudges me aside – and she has plenty to nudge me with, I can tell you.

'Not now. You do it to me in a minute.' I think she is probably right. It is better to concentrate on one thing at a time whether it be giving or receiving pleasure.

'Ooooooooooooooooooo oooooooooooooooooohhhhhh-hHHHH!!' No prizes for guessing who is giving tongue – if you'll excuse the expression. Miss B.'s marshmallow mouth wraps Percy in moist velvet and his happy owner croons in encouraging ecstasy.

'That's fantastic.' I stroke Miss B.'s head and can feel it rising and falling as if she is bobbing apples. Minutes pass in happy slurping before I feel an old-fashioned desire to play the gentleman.

'That's enough,' I murmur, 'I want to do it to you.'

I have never been a world champion muff diver but in the presence of such friendly service, how can I refuse?

I turn her on her back and send my north and south on a roller coaster ride down her switch-back body. This bird has more curves than a ton of hairpins and I have practically got a crick in my neck by the time I get down to her minge fringe. Natural delicacy and the National Viewers Council prevent me from describing the next few minutes in detail but if you have ever tried to untie a reef knot with your teeth while shooting Niagara Falls in a rubber dinghy you will get some idea of what I am up against. Talk about excited! This bint is practically coming apart at the seams. Just as I am beginning to wonder if they can hear her down at the guardroom she starts hauling me up her body like The Royal Standard – or, in my case, The Hammer and Suckle.

'Inside!' she barks, and it sounds as if she is talking to a wayward pooch that has been rooting in her rhododendrons. I am not slow to get her drift and in case I was, her mitts move swiftly to remind me of my responsibilities. She grabs Percy and surges forward so that I feel as if I am being thrown a lifebelt. Her not inconsiderable legs close around the small of my back and I can hear the referee counting 'One! Two! Three! Four! Five! Six!' – I struggle desperately but now I feel as if an enormous boa constrictor is swallowing me whole – 'Seven! Eight!' – forty thousand million sperm cells take a last bitter look at mum's photograph and prepare to go over the top – 'Nine! Ten! OUT!!' Now I begin to wonder whether they can hear *me* down at the guardroom.

Miss Bientot rumbles on like shunted goods wagons clinking away into the night and slowly releases her hold on me as she realizes that something beautiful has died between us, i.e. Percy.

'That was lovely,' she says. 'Now we must get the light working. There's a position on page three five two of that naughty book I find rather intriguing.'

CHAPTER SEVEN

When I struggle out of the library I am on hands and knees – and I wish to God they were someone else's hands and knees. To think I went to that bird to avoid falling into the hands of the military police. If I had known, I would have given myself up immediately. No wonder nobody ever goes to the bleeding library. They ought to warn you.

I am thinking about writing to my M.P. about it when I hear a low whistle coming from behind a pile of coke. I urge my whimpering loins forward and—

'Sidney! How did you get in here?'

'I climbed through a hole in the barbed wire.'

'Well show us where it is, for God's sake!' I find new strength to surge past him but am restrained by the arm that has lifted more buckshee pints than any other free loader in South London.

'What's the matter with you?' says Sid. 'You had enough, have you?'

'In a manner of speaking, yes Sid,' I say, glancing anxiously over my shoulder in case Miss Bientot reckons on taking a new lease on my life. 'What brings you here?'

'Sit down a minute,' says Sid considerately dusting a dent in the pile of coke. 'I came to ask you for some help.'

'What is it, Sid? How did you know I was going to be up here?' Whenever Sid asks for help I start getting nervous.

'Your mate, Ding Dong, told me you'd gone to change your library books. I didn't know you were much of a reader?'

'I'm not any more, it was just a phase I was going through. Now, come to the point, Sid. What can I possibly do to help you?'

Sidney shakes his head. 'I'm surprised at your tone,

Timmo. After being instrumental in bankrupting me I'd have thought you might have shown a little consideration.'

'Come off it, Sid! I'm very sorry about the caravan but I didn't have anything to do with it rolling down the hill. You should have got a bigger chock.'

'I beg your pardon!'

'I said "chock", Sidney.'

'Oh, good.' Sidney's face gets serious again. 'Now look, Timmo. Don't try and wriggle out of it. If you and your mates hadn't tried to storm the stage I might still be raking in the ackers and performing a social service to boot.'

'To boots, you mean, don't you? I wouldn't serve those old slags socially or otherwise.'

'That's not a very nice way to talk about talented thespians, Timmo.'

'They were thespians, were they?' I am surprised although I know that the acting profession is supposed to be a bit that way inclined. These three had looked quite normal as far as bedtime bagatelle was concerned.

'Yes, and they and I have been denied our livelihood, to say nothing of poor Vasco.'

I would be only too glad to be denied Vasco Snippet but I keep my thoughts to myself. I can see that Sidney is agitated.

'That fall opened up an old war wound,' he continues. 'Vasco is going to have to go back to Valetta.'

'She's not going to be very glad to see him in the state he was in when I left the vicarage.' 'War wound' indeed! I reckon he fought in the same war as my dad – the war against work.

'Valetta is the capital of Malta, you twit!' says Sidney, bitterly. 'Vasco was the last man to swim to freedom when the island was overrun by the Italians in the last war. Not unnaturally, he expected me to reimburse him.'

It seems very unnatural to me but you never know with these hot-blooded geezers, do you? Their ways are not our ways, as my Aunt Flo said when an Arab bloke showed her some photographs of his sister on a day trip to Port Said. Aunt Flo said she liked the flight but the place itself was disappointing. You couldn't get a decent cup of tea anywhere.

'I'm surprised you should do that, Sid.'

'Well, I didn't have much to give him,' says Sid with unusual truthfulness. 'He took all I had.'

I gaze at the pile of coke and keep my thoughts to myself. Something very strange has come over our Sidney.

'You're not expecting *me* to reimb—?' I don't like to say it somehow.

'No, Timmo. I know you've got even less than I have.'

I feel like arguing with him but, in the circumstances, it is in my interests to belt up. With Sidney on the turn and in the company of birds with thespian tendencies it is backs to the coke for everybody.

'I suppose you had to pay him off?' I say, deciding to change the subject.

'What do you think I've just been talking about, you berk! Of course I had to pay him off. That's why I'm skint. I had my last few bob tied up in that lot.'

'You've got your house at Vauxhall, Sid.'

'Only just. Have you heard of mortgages, Timmo? I can just see Rosie's face when I tell her we're moving out. She's chosen all the wallpaper. William Morris, it is.'

'I know the stuff. Got vintage cars all over it, hasn't it?'

Sidney closes his eyes and takes a deep, shuddering breath. Something seems to be disturbing him.

'Now that the caravan has gone we need somewhere to perform,' he says, slowly. 'I can't find anywhere in town and I haven't got any cash anyway. Between you and me, the girls are getting a bit nasty.'

I control myself with difficulty. 'They're still with you, are they?' Sidney nods.

'They haven't been paid, see? All the money went on Vasco and paying off the instalments on the caravan. The policy didn't cover it against being burnt in a barbecue pit.'

'What an elementary loop-hole,' I say. 'They're diabolical, some of these insurance companies.'

Sidney looks as if he is measuring my hooter for a bunch of fives and then thinks better of it.

'This place must be crawling with unused buildings,' he says meaningfully.

'What do you mean, Sid?' I say, knowing exactly what he means.

'Use your loaf, Timmo. If the blokes can't get to the show then bring the show to them.'

'Where do I come in?'

'That's the charm of it, Timmo. You don't have to come in. You're here already, aren't you? You know the lay of the land.'

'One or two of them,' I say nervously, looking towards the W.R.A.C.s lines as Percy gives a neurotic twitch.

'I mean, you'll be able to handle the internal organisation, find us somewhere to do the show and tell all the lads about it.'

'You must be joking, Sid.'

'I'll cut you in for a share, Timmo.'

'Sidney, I'd be in enough trouble if they knew I was at your last show, let alone organising a new one in the camp.'

Sidney allows a small smile to play round the corners of his mouth – frankly, I would never allow any small smile of mine to play in a place like that but you can't run other people's lives, can you?

'There's no reason why they should know,' he says.

'What do you mean?'

'Well, Timmo. If you won't play ball with me, I don't see why I should play ball with you. I might be tempted to let the M.P.s know that you were at our little entertainment.'

'Why should they believe you?'

Sidney's smile takes a stroll round his mug and he feels in his back pocket. 'Because I've got some pictorial evidence that you were there. There was some photographer geezer from the *Westery Chronicle* at the garden party and Vasco had the nous to nick his camera. Quite a nice one of you, this.'

I snatch the photograph from Sid's fingers and see that I do indeed share the foreground with one of Nora Nibbler's knockers.

'You can keep that for the family album if you like,' says Sid evilly, 'I've got lots of others. They're not all as flattering as that.'

'Blackmail, eh?' I accuse.

'Not blackmail, Timmo. That's a nasty word. I'm just trying to remind you of your family responsibilities. Blood is thicker than water, you know.'

'Let's check that,' I say.

'Put down that piece of coke, Timmo. Don't do anything silly. Look at it another way. How many blokes are there on this camp? A thousand. If we do two shows a night and get a hundred in each time at 50p, that's a hundred quid. A tenner each for the girls and you could be making thirty quid a night. That's nearly ten thousand a year for a six-day week, no tax and no V.A.T. Now, that's not bad, is it?'

'I'll have to think about it,' I say. 'Right, I've thought about it. When do we start?'

'Good thinking, Timmo. It was the family angle that finally got through to you, wasn't it?'

'Something like that. Tell you what, why don't we do four shows a day?'

I know I am being stupid but all that talk about money goes straight to my wallet – or it should do if I was dealing with anyone other than Sid. No matter how many times he does the dirty on me I never seem to learn.

'The girls won't wear it, Timmo. I've already asked them. How long is it going to take you to find us somewhere?'

'Not very long if it's costing me sixty quid a day.'

'Good, because they're getting a bit suspicious down at the Youth Hostel.'

'Youth Hostel?'

'Yeah. The girls don't like it much, I can tell you. The warden's always getting at them for the stiletto heel marks on his parquet floor. Stupid old sod. You should expect a bit of wear and tear if you're catering for nature lovers, shouldn't you?'

'Yes, Sid. But you don't go hiking in stiletto heels, do you?'

'Why not? They're very good for irritating the fields. That's what I told him anyway.'

Sid probably means 'irrigating' but I still have to hand it to him. Few blokes I know could keep three out and out scrubbers pinned down in the local Youth Hostel without them going stir crazy.

I reckon I am going to need some assistance so I sign up Tinker Bell and we have a little think about the best place to put on the show.

'I know just the spot,' he says, after a while. 'Nobody ever goes there.'

'The library? No, I don't reckon that for an idea. That bird could put us out of business in no time.'

'I didn't mean that. I was thinking about the church.'

'You can't do that. That's blasphemous. Imagine that bird and her— No I can't be having that.'

I mean, I never go to church but that doesn't mean that I don't have a lot of religious convictions – as well as my two for lead-stripping and appearing in a blue movie I didn't know was being made.

'Let me finish! I was thinking about the church hall. That's not religious, is it?'

'Not so religious. And it's near the edge of the camp as well.'

The ramshackle tin hut behind the church is certainly

a better bet. No chance of Tita Lotof bursting out of the font or anything distasteful like that.

'What do they use it for?'

'Nothing, as far as I know. They used to have a cub pack there but that was disbanded about the same time as the padre was defrocked.'

'Yeah. I remember seeing a picture of the frock in the papers.'

'Didn't do a lot for him, did it?'

'Not with those Army boots, no. Anyway, I reckon we've found the new Club On Wheels.'

'We can't call it that any more. We'll have to have a new name.'

'Yeah. And something that won't arouse suspicion. I know, we'll call it The Mess, short for Magically Erotic Sexy Striptease.'

Tinker can be quite smart sometimes and he is also good at forcing windows. All in all I am glad I am paying him two quid per hundred customers.

Later that evening we recce the joint and find that there is even a stage in it. The curtain doesn't work so well and half the benches are broken but we are far from choked. The fewer the seats, the more room there is for standing customers. We get word to Sid that accommodation has been found and draw him a plan to show where the hut is. Seven o'clock the following evening is agreed as the time of the first show and Tinker and I start dashing about like blue-arsed flies selling tickets. Our biggest problem is that nobody takes us seriously. They are so crushed by the system that they can only think about bulling up their boots for the following morning's kit inspection. The more technicolour aspects of life's rich tapestry seem to be beyond their ken.

'How are they going to get past the guardroom?' asks Loogy when we tell him the good news.

'Up your arse,' says Sculthorpe who has not enlarged his

vocabulary since our map reading – and Percy stretching – exercise.

'Come, come, lads,' I reassure them. 'I'm dead serious. At nineteen hundred hours that hut behind the church is going to be full of quivering crumpet all set to drive you clean out of your Y-fronts.'

One of the many hard men in the billet feels, almost reluctantly, in his back pocket. 'It had better be. Otherwise, you're going to be dead – serious. Get me?'

He nearly drives a 50p piece through the palm of my hand and I give him one of my weaker smiles. Sidney had better show up on time otherwise I will be up shit creek without adequate navigational equipment.

The afternoon passes in a merry riot of P.T., arms drill and assault courses and it is all I can do to get off my bed as nineteen hundred hours approaches.

'Better get down there and see that everything is all right,' says Bell. 'We don't want any slip-ups.'

Never was a truer word spoken and I congratulate myself upon having such an astute and conscientious assistant. I do that mainly so that I can demonstrate that I know what words like 'astute' and 'conscientious' mean.

The Mess is not far from the perimeter wire and near the scrubland that leads out to the rifle ranges. Bell and I approach it from the camp side and I am about to give him a leg up to one of the windows when we hear a horse whinny from the other side of the building. Round we go with our hearts in our chests – nothing abnormal about us – and there are two horses tethered to a tree and munching that green stuff you see a lot of in public parks. No sooner have we made our discovery than a low moan alerts us to the fact that there is human life in the Mess. Maybe Sidney has rolled up early and is killing a few minutes with one of the cast. I would not have reckoned him as being the horsey type but it must be better than walking.

'Take a dekko through the window,' says Tinker. 'If

there's someone in there we've got to get rid of them and pronto!'

I lift myself up and – blimey! They were the last couple I would have reckoned on doing something like that to each other. When I catch a glimpse of *An Anthology of Eastern Love Arts* propped against one of their riding boots I get an idea of where the inspiration is coming from. Cool, upper-class Lieutenant Bland and little Amanda Nasty are tucking into each other with the vigour of someone trying to suck a plateful of spaghetti through a megaphone.

'Oh, how absolutely spiffing!' Barmy's muffled – and I mean muffled – voice comes leaking through to me and he takes a swift butchers at the instruction manual.

'I say, this one looks rather fun. The position of the inverted lotus. It's supposed to be for chaps with one leg and pregnant women but we might give it a go, what?'

I return to Tinker's side feeling double choked. I never like to see a bird I have tangled with having it away with someone else. It seems almost indecent somehow. I reckon that after me they should go into a convent and meditate on the beauty of the experience for the rest of their naturals. Seeing her indulging in a spot of nasty munching has quite upset me.

'What's going on in there?' says Tinker.

'Just about everything, mate. Barmy and Major Nasty's daughter are on the job.'

'I'd better have a look—'

'Come back here, you crude sod! They're not doing anything you haven't dreamt about.' I pull Bell away from the window and try to get him to concentrate on the job in hand.

'Unless we can get them out of there in the next couple of minutes we're going to be in dead schtuck. If Sculthorpe and his mates come along and find there isn't a show they're going to have our guts for garters. Now, what are we going to do?'

'Set fire to the place.'

'What a brilliant idea. Now why didn't I think of that? It's made of tin so there's nothing to set light to and if we did burn it down there'd be nowhere to have the show. Have you thought of asking for a transfer to the Intelligence Corps?'

'Have you got a better idea, Einstein?'

I don't get a chance to tell him because a stooped figure wearing an old Army greatcoat with the collar turned up appears at our side.

'Is this the bleeding place?' pants Sid. 'I hope nobody ever asks you two berks to draw a map. I ended up in the W.R.A.C. Sergeants' Mess. They're a fruity load of cows, aren't they? I was no sooner inside the door than—'

'You don't have to tell us, Sid. We know. Now, where are the girls?'

Sid looks uncomfortable. 'You haven't taken any money yet, have you?'

'Of course we have. We didn't want a blooming great queue building up, did we? We sold all the tickets in advance and told the blokes to show them as they went in. They should be rolling up any minute.'

'Oh, my gawd!' Sid buries his face in his hands.

'What's the matter, Sid? Where are the girls?' I am not surprised to hear a mounting strain of hysteria invading my voice.

'They're peeling potatoes back at the Youth Hostel.'

'They're what!?'

'The warden got all narky because they hadn't made their beds or helped sweep out the dormitory. He's not letting them out 'til they've done all the spuds for the next three days.'

'He can't do that!'

'He's done it, mate. When I looked through the window I couldn't see them over the pile of spuds. It's no good. You'll have to give everyone their money back.'

'You don't understand, Sid. If these blokes don't get some action they're going to tear us apart. We had a lot of trouble convincing them we were on the level in the first place.'

'We're going to be under the level when Sculthorpe and his mates get here,' says Tinker. 'Let's grab those horses and make a bolt for it.'

'I didn't know you blokes were in the cavalry,' says Sid. 'Can you give us a lift to the perimeter wire?'

'They don't belong to us, Sid. They belong to the couple who are on the job in there.'

'On the job?' says Sidney, and I can see the germ of an idea beginning to infect his face. 'They wouldn't fancy a few bob to throw it open to the public, would they?'

'I don't reckon they need it. It's our platoon commander and his bird.'

'Platoon commander? That's not right. That's disgusting, that is.'

Before you can say 'Blackmail' Sid has stepped smartly to the door of the hut and thrown it open.

'Right. Don't move, you'll do yourselves an injury.' I don't know whether they are still on the inverted lotus but whatever it is they must be in good physical shape to get themselves into *that* position.

'What the devil do you think you're doing?' sings out Barmy, protecting his python with his riding boots.

'I might ask you the same question,' says Sid producing a small camera from his greatcoat pocket. 'Hardly a good example for young soldier boys, is it?'

He snaps away while Barmy tries to struggle into Amanda's panties.

'Put that camera away!' squeals Miss Nasty making no effort to conceal her furry charms.

'Don't bother to put your clothes on,' says Sid. 'You've got work to do.'

'What do you mean? Who are you?' yelps Amanda.

'If you don't put on a show for the blokes who are coming in here in the next few minutes, I'm going to splash these photographs all over the camp. Your chances of getting to Badminton won't be worth a tossed shuttlecock.'

'A show?'

'You know what I mean. A few more like you were doing when we came in.'

'How dare you!'

'Common little blackmailer!'

'They're coming, Sid.' Sculthorpe's ugly frame can be seen stalking across the grass.

'You've got thirty seconds to get behind that curtain,' says Sid coldly.

'I won't do it,' says Barmy.

'Not even for the lady's sake?' reproves Sid. 'That's not very gentlemanly.'

'Don't talk to me about being "gentlemanly",' howls Barmy.

'Fifteen seconds,' says Sid.

'But they'll recognise us,' says Amanda.

'Cut your tights in half and pull them over your faces like masks. Hey, you, Ding Dong. Take them behind that bleeding curtain and get them fixed up.'

'It's impossible. I can't possibly—' Barmy is still protesting as Amanda leads him away behind the curtain. Women always seem to react better to the unexpected than men.

'Get those benches lined up!' Sidney is making Cecil B. de Mille seem like a nervous vicar running his first knobbly knees contest. No sooner has he danced up onto the stage than Sculthorpe, Loogy and the rest of the barrack room push into the hut.

'It's not exactly the London Palladium, is it?' sniffs Loogy.

'When this show starts you won't be looking at the scenery, sonny,' sings out Sidney. 'I'm not certain that we haven't gone too far this time. If it's too explicit, leave quietly and we'll give you your money back.'

'Bollocks!' says Sculthorpe. 'You're never going to shock me.'

'I wish I had a couple of thousand volts handy to prove you wrong, son,' says Sidney unpleasantly.

The hut is filling up fast and I am kept at full stretch checking the tickets. I only hope that Barmy is in the same extended condition.

'Right lads, tonight's show marks a breakthrough in forces entertainment and is an attempt to portray to you the ultimate in sexual ecstasy that can be obtained by two young people who are not ashamed of their bodies or the impulses that generate in them a frank and beautiful desire—'

'Get on with it!'

'Belt up, short arse!!' Sidney obviously does not take kindly to interruption. 'One more crack out of you and you'll get a bunch of fives up your hooter.'

A dignified silence falls on the company.

'—to delve into the innermost recesses of that rich store of physical experience which is the hallmark of the totally liberated man and woman of the seventies.' Somebody farts loudly and Sidney pauses for a moment before deciding to ignore this latest assault on good taste. 'Gentlemen, I give you "Freedom to love – Army style".'

We all look towards the stage and there is a moment's pause while the curtain refuses to budge. It gives a couple of petulant trembles and then collapses on the top of what are presumably two heaving bodies stretched out on a trestle table. Tinker steps forward to expose the dynamic duo but only succeeds in collapsing one end of the table so that its occupants slide to the floor in an untidy heap. An ugly guffaw rises from the body of the hall. Sidney curses and his mood does not improve when the curtain is eventually removed.

'I said "separate the tights"!' he hollers. 'Gordon Bennett, did you ever seen anything like it?'

It is a regrettable fact that Barmy and Amanda are face to face for no other reason than that their bonces are jammed into the same pair of tights.

'At least they put them in separate legs,' I say, trying to look on the bright side.

'Give over! That blooming mate of yours must be round the twist. Get up there and sort them out.'

Amanda and Barmy are trying to climb to their feet but it is difficult when you can't see anything and they topple over the collapsed table. From what I can see Barmy is not in peak condition to give a royal command performance and I can't really blame him.

'Don't let them see my face,' he bleats pathetically as I look round for something to separate the couple.

The audience have been shouting the place down but suddenly there is a hush like that which falls over Anfield Road when the opposition score a goal. I turn round to see that Sidney is trying to stop a group of determined-looking ladies from pushing their way into the hut.

'I'm sorry,' he is saying firmly. 'No ticket, no admittance. You have to pay your 50p like everybody else.'

'How dare you!! What is going on here? Do you know who I am?' The lady who is making with the chat gives Sidney six inches and looks as if no one has ever returned the compliment.

'I don't care if you're the Queen of Sheba, duckie. It's 50p or no see.'

'I'm Mrs Runcorn and these ladies are fellow members of the camp dramatic society.'

'They look like fellows, and all, some of them,' says Sid, unkindly. 'I'm sorry, there's no reduction for trade.'

'Mrs Runcorn,' croaks Amanda. 'Oh my goodness. She's the C.O.'s wife.'

Down in the body of the hall blokes are diving through windows like it is a frog barbecue and Sidney must be bonkers if he does not get the message that this place is less healthy than a game of tag in a leper colony.

'Who are you?' snarls Mrs Runcorn, 'and what is going on in—' Her beady eyes flash past me to collide with Amanda's big end. 'Good Gracious!!'

'Run for it,' I shout.

Standing behind Mrs Runcorn is Miss A. Bientot and she is staring straight at me.

Something in her eyes tells me that I will be expected to change my library books in the very near future.

CHAPTER EIGHT

'I thought it was amazing how they both got on the horse,' says Tinker.

'It didn't half go, didn't it?' says Loogy admiringly.

The discussion concerns the sight of Amanda and Barmy disappearing at speed towards the rifle range, still wearing Amanda's tights.

'Were they going to use the horse in the act?' says Loogy, hopefully.

'I don't think so,' I tell him.

'The other bloke hadn't ridden much.'

This is indeed true. In fact I find it difficult to recall a single occasion on which Sidney has straddled a gee-gee in my presence. Small wonder that his greatcoat was found inextricably enmeshed in the perimeter wire – with the horse grazing two fields away.

'When are we getting our money back?'

This is a question I have been asked a number of times since the show; not often so civilly.

'As soon as we see our partner we'll get the money back, don't you worry.'

'I'm not worried,' says the bloke.

'Well, you should be,' I think to myself. Knowing Sid's spending habits I don't reckon there is much chance of seeing any change from the hundred quid we gave him. That being the case, my chances of not being duffed up by disappointed patrons are less than that of an overweight turkey showing up at a New Year's Eve party.

'I'd be quite happy to see the show again,' says Loogy. 'It looked a bit of all right, did that.'

'I don't think we'd ever be able to retain the same artistes,'

I say. 'They're booked up a long way in advance.' And still riding, I reckon.

In fact Barmy shows up wearing his uniform and pink cheeks at our next drill parade. He does not say much and I notice that he is walking with a slight limp, but at least he is still in one piece.

Two days later the whole company is in one of the lecture rooms and I look around nervously for M.P.s. For every minute of the last forty-eight hours I have been expecting to be dragged squealing to the guardroom and I reckon that this could be the big purge.

Major Nasty stalks in looking like the before part of a stomach powder advertisement and we are called to attention.

'Thank you, Sergeant Major. At ease, sit down. Now, I expect you are all wondering why you have been assembled here. The answer is quite simple: we are going to attack the Americans.'

'I knew it.' says Tinker. 'Once we started getting friendly with the Ruskies and the Chinks something like this was a blooming certainty.'

All around us there is considerable unhappiness at the Major's news. There is a lot of difference between being in the Army and having people shoot at you. With guns. Real guns.

'Of course,' continues Major Nasty, 'I am referring to an exercise.' Everybody smiles and nods at each other. Of course, we all knew he was talking about an exercise, didn't we?

'The C.O. has agreed with Colonel Mandervilliers of The Flying Sky Tigers that we should check out the camp's defensive system by launching a mock attack during a predetermined period of time. As you know, R.A.F. Great Little Missingham is the home of the Sky Tigers and one of the bulwarks of the N.A.T.O. defence system. If we ever – and God forbid that this day should ever come – have to strike back at an aggressor then the counterblow will come from Great Little Missingham.'

'I had a counterblow once,' says Tinker. 'I was working in Sainsbury's and there was this fantastic bird on the bacon slicer—'

'Belt up,' I tell him. I mean, this is what it is all about, isn't it? Adventure, excitement, and still no chance of getting your balls shot off.

'This is a chance for you chaps to show what you can do,' says Nasty. 'So far your training has been strictly academic. Now it enters a new phase. Your platoon commanders will brief you on the details of the plan of attack. All I want to say is good luck and remember what those Yankee scum were doing to your wives and sweethearts during the war.'

'I reckon he must mean his wife and sweetheart,' says Tinker. 'My bird wasn't born 'til ten years after the war.'

'Maybe it was your mum they were doing it to,' I suggest.

'Don't be filthy. My mum never had it away with anyone.'

'What are you then? Some kind of immaculate contraception?'

'Belt up, you two!!' Sergeant Lake's voice snuffs out our voices like a D.D.T. aerosol.

'That's very interesting,' says Sid when we tell him the news. 'Very interesting indeed.'

We are sitting in a café in Westery and Sid is thoughtfully fiddling with one of the many pieces of sticking plaster that criss-cross his mug like they are holding together a cracked window pane. The subject of horse-riding has been avoided but there seems little doubt that Sidney will not be putting in an early seat application for The Horse Of The Year Show.

'I've been thinking a lot about that air base recently,' continues Sid. 'Those Yanks have a lot of money, you know.'

'Yeah, and they've got a lot of things to spend it on and all.'

'Not at Great Little Missingham, they haven't. It's one of these top security bases and the blokes aren't let off the camp. All the entertainment has to come in to them.'

'I expect they do all right.'

'I know just the opposite,' says Sid with feeling. 'This bloke Mandervilliers is as straight as a Hashamite's hampton. He wouldn't allow the Women's Institute in there to give them a poetry reading. They're all on an ice cream-free diet and their hair is only just allowed to show through the top of their nuts. If ever a group of blokes were ripe for a spot of mature entertainment, it's them.'

'But you can't get in.'

'I *couldn't* get in. Now I reckon that fate may have intervened to show me the way. I'm a great believer in fate, Timmo. Whenever things go badly for a while I always know that something is going to turn up.'

I wish I could be as certain. I haven't seen a lot of upward nudges on Sid's fortune curve recently.

'I don't see what you're on about,' says Bell.

'You blokes are going to make a raid on the camp, right?' says Sid, patiently. 'Now the way I look at it, if me and the birds can come along for the ride, we'll be able to get inside the camp, no trouble.'

'You must be barmy. I doubt if *we're* going to be able to get into the camp, let alone cart you along for the ride.'

'The Yanks know you're going to attack them, don't they?'

'Yeah, but they don't know when or how.'

'They will do. You tell me and I'll tell my contacts and they'll be no trouble. We'll be in there like a dose of salts and then on with the show.'

' "We"?'

'You don't want to be left out of this one, do you, Timmo?' Sid's mug assumes an expression of helpless amazement. 'These Yanks are so loaded they don't know what to do with it. And they're crying out for a whiff of crumpet. We'll make more out of one show than we might have made out of a month with your lot.'

'If they find out, they'll put us inside and throw away the key.'

'But they won't find out. The very unusualness of the scheme will ensure its success. Nobody would expect a strip-tease show to be attacking an air base.'

'You've got a point there, Sidney. Do you think the girls will play ball?'

'They'll play with anyone's balls, mate. Especially after being cooped up in that barn.'

'What barn, Sid? I thought they were in the Youth Hostel.'

An expression of pain creeps across Sid's face. 'We had a bit of trouble there. Very unfortunate.'

'What happened, Sid?'

'Young Curates' Cycling Club rolled up. Nice lads, they were, some of them. Led very sheltered lives, you know what I mean? The girls were getting a bit – how shall I put it?'

'Frustrated, Sid?'

'Yeah. Frustrated sort of gets the flavour of it. They'd finished all the spuds and you know what they say: the Devil finds work for ideal hands to do.'

'I have heard something like that, Sid.'

'Nora, I think it was Nora, got hold of a bottle of cooking sherry – she likes a drop, does Nora – and in no time they're away. The poor little curates were piling their beds against the dormitory door but it didn't do any good. The lucky ones are still pedalling across the Malvern Hills.'

'Nasty, Sid.'

'Very nasty. And the warden didn't like it, I can tell you. He tore up their membership cards and told them never to darken his tea towels again. I tried to reason with him but it didn't do any good. "Girls will be girls," I said. "You're only young once." But he didn't want to know. "What about all these surplus surplices? Where am I going to send them?" That was all he could think about. That and the cassocks. Bloody stupid stuff to go cycling in if you ask me. I reckon they were asking for trouble.'

'So you're in a barn now, Sid?'

'Well I'm not in the bleeding country club, am I? Use your common.'

'Looks like that's what you could be doing next, Sid.'

'What are you on about?'

'Using your common, Sid. You see, if you get kicked out of the barn you'll have to—'

'Belt up! Don't give me any of your rotten jokes. I'm not in the mood for them. I'm racked with rheumatism and raked with barbed wire and I don't want to know. Now, let's hear what you know about this bleeding attack.'

* * *

Two days later I am climbing on board a fire engine. Yes, that's right, a fire engine. Some blooming genius has decided that we will take the Yanks by surprise if we roll up at the main gate of Great Little Missingham in three fire engines, ringing bells and making like the base is on fire. The Yanks will let us through and our fathers' wives and sweethearts will be avenged. Major Nasty is so excited about the plan that he actually smiles when he describes it. You can see his mug splitting into uncertain creases like a piece of freshly folded cardboard.

Sergeant Lake is sitting beside the driver of our fire engine and Bell and I are on the back. Fortunately we are at the rear of the convoy.

'I'm scared,' says Tinker as we speed along the narrow lanes. 'Do we have to go through with it?'

'Not unless you mind Sid showing all those photographs of us to the C.O. He's got quite a nice selection now, you know. He took a few more in the tin hut.'

'Oh my Gawd. Where are we supposed to pick them up?'

'Not far now. About another mile down the road after we've crossed the ford.'

I peer round the side of the driver's cab and try and stop

my helmet from falling over my eyes. In a few minutes something should happen.

Splash! We hit the ford and the driver stabs at his brakes as we come out the other side. Hardly has he put his foot on the accelerator again than a riderless bike glides out of the hedgerow. Crash! The fire engine brakes hard but the bike is under the front wheels before you can say Crunch Time.

'What the bleeding hell—!!'

'Get your foot out of my earhole.'

Everybody starts shouting and we crowd round the bonnet. 'Where's the bloke gone?'

'Can you see him, Sarge?'

Lakey drops to his knees and peers under the chassis. No sooner has he sunk below hub cap level than Sid and the birds flash out of the undergrowth and jump onto the back of the fire engine.

'Hey!' says one sharp-eyed git. 'What do you think—?'

'Belt up! They're friends of ours and we're giving them a lift. Want to make something of it?' Tinker Bell's mug shivers menacingly a few inches away from the protester's hooter.

'No, of course not.'

'The others aren't waiting for us, Sarge,' I say.

Sergeant Lake scrambles to his feet. 'If that's someone's idea of a joke I'd like to get my hands on them.' He turns to the driver. 'Drive over it. Come on the rest of you, get mounted. We haven't got any time to lose. Come on! MOVE!!'

'Ooh, I wish he wouldn't shout like that,' says Loogy. 'His voice goes right through me. It's fun this, isn't it? I always wanted to have a ride on a fire engine when I was a kid.' He smiles at Trixie Bigun who looks at him like he is a ladder in a new pair of tights. 'You come along for the ride, have you?'

Trixie ungums her pillarbox red lips and tells him to piss off.

None of the ladies seem in particularly high spirits and if the pong they are giving off is anything to go by one can see why. Talk about Cattle No. 5. I have not niffed anything like it since Mum cooked a steam pudding in one of Dad's vests. The girls are all wearing plastic macs which serve as windows through which one can see the acres of bare flesh underneath. Not very warm, though.

'How much longer?' says Tinker nervously.

No sooner has he spoken than the fire engine bell starts ringing and I see the perimeter wire of the airbase beginning to flash past.

'Excited, girls?' says Sid.

'You must be soft in the head,' says Tita Lotof. The other girls are less friendly.

'If I don't get some money this time, I'm going to Equity,' says Nora.

'It's very nice,' says Loogy. 'My sister took her kids there once. If you like an outdoor holiday—'

'Do us a favour, Loogy. We've got enough problems at the moment.'

'Get ready to jump off when I tell you,' warns Sidney.

The fire engine lurches to the left and we sweep through the gates of the airbase. I catch a glimpse of geezers in helmets squatting behind piles of sandbags and imagine that they must be part of the defensive forces. They look up at us without showing much interest and it seems as if Nasty's master plan is working.

'Right, at the next corner. Here we go!'

The fire engine slows down a fraction and Sidney's party launches itself into space.

'Do you know where we are, Sid?'

'Pretty well. I've got a map somewhere.' Sidney pats his chest and shakes his head. 'That's the trouble with these bleeding smocks: no pockets.'

'Still it suits you, Sid. You look a right little Walter Gabriel.'

'Don't take the piss, Timmo. If you had my problems to

overcome, you wouldn't even be here.'

'Too true, I wouldn't. I wouldn't be here if I didn't have your problems to overcome.'

'Stop rabbiting and help Nora out of that flower bed. Her tassels are getting soaked.'

We straggle after Sid and I suddenly hear a fusillade of shots. The attack must have begun in Ernest – or some other poor sod.

'Hey! You guys. Leg it over here. This is where the action is.' A sleepy-voiced Yank is talking to us from the doorway of a hut.

'Abe. Good to see you. Let's get inside and I'll introduce you to everyone.' Sidney shepherds us off the pathway and Abe brushes me aside to get a handful of the girls. From the look in his eyes I can see what Sid was getting at. The way he squeezes Tita's forearm suggests that it would be unwise to leave him alone with my grandma's neutered tom.

'You sure are beautiful,' he mumbles dragging his eyes over her boobs like they are suction cleaners snatching up pieces of unwanted clothing.

'I may be just an old Texas longhorn but I sure in tarnation know a lovely gal when I see one.'

'Any long horn is a friend of mine,' breathes Tita sincerely. 'That accent of yours drives me out of my mind.'

I would not have thought it would get crowded enough in there to start a migration but I hold my peace. Tex Ritter is trying to hold my piece as well.

'How about you and me moseying over to the soda fountain,' he trills. 'I've got somebody I'd like to introduce you to. He's got a couple of round, chubby, little friends and they'd sure like to meet you.'

I am beginning to wonder about the identity of the mysterious stranger when Sidney moves in swiftly.

'No snaffling the goodies,' he says waving what I believe is known as an admonishing finger. 'My little girls haven't come just to entertain you. Where are those Sky Tiger Stags you were telling me about?'

'Shucks. I was just checking over the merchandise,' chortles Abe giving one of Tita's titties a playful tweak. 'The rest of the fellows are waiting in the Glade.'

'The Glade?'

'That's where the Stags hang out.' He jerks his thumb toward a partition from behind which I can hear noises like a Tottenham Hotspur F.C. Supporters' Club special pulling into Euston three hours late. I apply my eye to a convenient peep-hole and snatch a butchers at a bunch of blokes in sun vizors and shirt sleeves who are looking tense and expectant. Many of them have bottles clasped in their brawny mits and they do not look like they enter for a lot of croquet tournaments.

'Where do we change?' says Trixie.

'Right over here, sweetheart,' says Abe, an expectant smile starting to spread over his face.

'What do you mean "change"?' snarls Sid. 'You've only got to take your plastic macs off. What do you think this is? The Royal Command Performance?'

'You're a pig!' sniffs Nora. 'You treat us like muck. I want proper facilities or I'm not going through with it.'

'See what I'm up against?' moans Sid. 'Fifth rate performers with star temperament. And to think I found this bird in a massage parlour.'

'I found you in a massage parlour, you mean. It's the worst thing I ever did. I should have known what you were like when you asked me to—'

'That's enough about that,' says Sidney hurriedly. 'Are you going to discharge your contractual obligations or aren't you?'

'Talking filthy isn't going to make me do anything,' says Nora with feeling – most of which is coming from Abe. 'Get your hands off me!'

'Have you got anywhere else the girls can change?' says Sidney, wearily.

'Nope. Might be able to lay hands on a few screens from the Rankers' Rest Room.'

'The what?!' says Sidney.

'He said "Rankers", Sidney.'

'I'm glad to hear it. I knew that they had it cushy in the Yank army but – blimey!'

'I'd show you where to find them but I guess I'd better stay here and tell the guys what's happening. Some of them are getting a little restless.' The sound of shattering glass gives us an idea of what he is talking about.

'You come with me, Timmy. The rest of you stay there. We'll be back in a couple of minutes, Dame Sybil. You practice your electrocution.'

'Don't you mean elocution?' I say as we go out through the door.

'Not in her case, Timmo. The sooner she practices her high wire act on a power cable the better as far as I'm concerned.'

We start walking down the road towards a large N.A.A.F.I.-type building and I can hear bursts of gunfire coming from the centre of the camp. I hope they are using blanks.

'Yooo Hoooo! Come and get me!' Standing at the doorway of a whitewood house is a tall redhead wearing slacks and sun glasses. Her hair is freshly coiffeured and she has a drink in her hand. Something tells me that she could spell trouble – she'd have to be pretty stupid not to be able to, wouldn't she?

'What do you want?' says Sidney irritably.

'I want to give myself up. Surrender. Lay down my arms.' The lady stretches out both those items invitingly.

'She's pissed,' says Sidney. 'Leave her alone. We've got a job to do.'

'Invade me,' urges the lady. 'Where's all that rape and pillage I've been dreaming of?'

'Come on!' urges Sid.

'Don't run away, boys. Surely we can have a little shot before you go?'

Not wishing to totally disappoint the lady I raise my rifle in the air and discharge a blank.

'I meant a shot of bourbon, Tovarich. God, how did you guys ever invent the Sputnik?'

'She's round the twist,' says Sidney. 'Come on. We've got to get those screens.'

The bint disappears into the house and I start to turn away.

'You like guns, I like guns.' I turn back just as there is a sharp crack and something bends the air beside my lughole. The lady now has a pistol in her hand and it is pointing at us.

'I was only firing a blank,' I yelp.

'I wasn't. Come and have that drink.'

Sidney and I practically lock our shoulders in the doorway.

'Don't you think you'd better put that thing down?' I humour her. 'After all, you are our prisoner.'

'Not until you've done what you're supposed to do. An unprotected female has got rights in a situation like this. I expect to be raped and if you two guys know what's good for you you'll sure as hell start raping.' A bullet bisects the distance between us and there is the sound of shattering glass.

'We can't do it here,' pleads Sidney.

The bird looks at him intently and for a moment I think she is going to shoot him.

'You're right,' she says finally. 'Alvin and Debbie will be back from school soon. It wouldn't be very nice. I remember my psychiatrist saying something about it. And then, of course, there's poor Alvin Senior.' She looks down at a framed photograph on a fireside table and I see a geezer with so much medal ribbon on his chest that it looks like a wall chart of international flags. What also strikes my eye is the name tag: Mandervilliers.

'Is that your husband?' I ask, my stomach beginning to decide which leg to slide down.

'Yes. That's Alvin. And I'm Miranda Mandervilliers. It's a cute name, isn't it?' She starts to hold out her hand and then checks herself. 'Shucks! It's going to spoil the whole deal if we know each other too well before you rape me. Come on, I know just the spot. I've always wanted to be raped there. It's kind of auspicious if you know what I mean.'

'Look, couldn't we—?'

'Start moving.' Mrs Mandervilliers' pop gun is pointing straight at Percy and he starts moving so fast that the rest of me has to run to catch up.

'Gawd, we don't half have some bleeding bad luck,' says Sidney. 'A few more capers like this and I'm going to pack the whole thing in.'

Out of the back of the house we go and through a small garden with a gate in the fence at the end of it. This leads into a clump of trees. In their midst is an isolated building with a jeep outside. Mrs M. marches up to the sentry and acknowledges his salute.

'I'm going downstairs,' she says as if she doesn't expect to be argued with. The sentry looks at Sid and myself suspiciously. 'Ma'am, are you sure the Colonel—?'

'Yes!'

We go down a long flight of stairs and there is another guard and another door.

'I'm going to be knackered before we get there,' I whisper to Sid.

'I don't like this,' he says. 'I don't like it at all.'

Mrs M. says something to the guard and the door slides open. Beyond it is a dimly lit room with a table and chair in the middle of it. A soldier with an automatic rifle is sitting by the far wall gazing at a button set in the middle of it.

'What's that for?' I ask Mrs M.

'Room service,' she snaps. 'O.K., soldier. You can wait outside.'

'But my orders—'

'Screw your orders! Beat it!!'

The soldier looks as if he is going to say something then shrugs his shoulders and goes out.

'O.K. you Cossacks, defile me.'

'But—'

'Don't argue with her, Sid. The quicker we can get this over, the quicker we can get back for those screens.'

Seizing Mrs Mandervilliers by the shoulder I push her back onto the table and kiss her like I am trying to autograph her epiglottis with my tongue. Sid releases her slacks and pulls them down over her knees. Blimey! That woman must have been belting back the booze. A couple more kisses and I reckon I would be pissed myself.

'Mercy, mercy!' moans Mrs M. 'Show me no mercy!'

I start unbuttoning her blouse and have revealed that her Yanky doodles are dandy when I hear Sid's zipper tracing the lower register.

'I find this very embarrassing,' he says. 'The things you have to do to run a business these days.'

'It's all right, Sid. I won't watch.' I concentrate on the lady's bristols and can feel her whole body heaving as Sidney starts stoking the boiler.

'OOOOOOOOOOOH!!' The lady suddenly lets out an enormous whoop of relief and her head falls back against the table.

'What's happened!?'

'I think she's passed out.'

'Oh my gawd! What are we going to do?'

'Ring that bell. That'll bring someone.' I cross the room with Elliot Ness swiftness and reach for the bell push.

'DON'T MOVE!!'

Framed in the doorway I can make out Colonel Mandervilliers, Major Nasty, Sergeant Lake and a cast of thousands all of whom carry weapons which are pointed at my heart.

Sidney is still standing between Miranda's legs and he steps back bashfully before speaking.

'This wasn't our idea,' he says.

CHAPTER NINE

'Eight Russian cities,' says Sidney. 'Blimey. It makes you think, doesn't it?'

'And all by pushing that little button. Shows how careful you've got to be, doesn't it?'

'I could see what the bloke was upset about. Not just his wife but wiping out half of western civilisation. I mean, I'd have been bit narky if I'd been him.'

'Definitely. He's got a job to do.'

'And it can't be very easy with a wife like that.'

'Funny woman, wasn't she?'

'Very.'

'Still it's a good job she's the way she is, otherwise I wouldn't have got my dishonourable discharge so easily.'

'Too true, Timmo. It wouldn't have looked very nice in the papers, would it?'

'I'm sorry about the skiing, though.'

'Yeah, but nine years is a long time to have to hang about just on the off chance. I've got a little idea that might bring the whole thing a lot nearer.'

'Importing snow?'

'No, Timmo. I mean loot-wise. You've heard of the Supremes, haven't you?'

'Naturally.'

'Well, how do you see Trixie, Tita and Nora as Britain's answer to Jamjar Lowdown or whatever it is?'

'You mean Tamla Motown, Sid. Frankly, I don't. In fact I haven't seen them at all since we left The Glade.'

Sidney finishes his scotch and wipes his mouth with the back of his hand as he looks around for the waiter.

'Blimey, you're right. They're probably still there. Still, in the circumstances—' He thumbs through an impressive roll of dollar bills '—it's good to know they're giving value for money. We'll have to find three more girls. I definitely think there's money in this pop business, Timmo. Waiter, two more large scotches, please.'

If Sidney is buying double scotches he must believe it. 'Do you fancy anything?' he says to me.

'I'll have the same, thanks, Sid.'

'Make that four double scotches, waiter.' Sid winks at me and the train goes into the tunnel.